The Green Gables Detectives

D0012607

Books by Eric Wilson

The Tom and Liz Austen Mysteries

1. Murder on *The Canadian*
2. Vancouver Nightmare
3. The Case of the Golden Boy
4. Disneyland Hostage
5. The Kootenay Kidnapper
6. Vampires of Ottawa
7. Spirit in the Rainforest
8. The Green Gables Detectives
9. Code Red at the Supermall
10. Cold Midnight in Vieux Québec
11. The Ice Diamond Quest
12. The Prairie Dog Conspiracy
13. The St. Andrews Werewolf
14. The Inuk Mountie Adventure
15. Escape from Big Muddy

Also available by Eric Wilson

Summer of Discovery
The Unmasking of 'Ksan
Terror in Winnipeg
The Lost Treasure of Casa Loma
The Ghost of Lunenburg Manor

The Green Gables Detectives

A Liz Austen Mystery

by

ERIC WILSON

HarperCollins*PublishersLtd*

This book is for Rick Hansen,
the triumphant "Man in Motion."

The author appreciates the kind assistance of the Government of P.E.I., Department of Tourism. Special thanks to Lloyd McKenna. The author and the publisher thank Ruth Macdonald and David Macdonald for permission to make use of characters and events from Anne of Green Gables *by L.M. Montgomery. ANNE OF GREEN GABLES is a trademark of the heirs of L.M. Montgomery. A share of the royalties from* The Green Gables Detectives *is being contributed to the L.M. Montgomery P.E.I. Children's Literature Award.*

As in his other mysteries, Eric Wilson writes here about imaginary people in a real landscape.

Find Eric Wilson at http://hypbus.com/ewilson/

THE GREEN GABLES DETECTIVES. Copyright © 1987 by Eric Hamilton Wilson. All rights reserved. No part of this book may be used or reproduced in any manner whatsoever without prior written permission except in the case of brief quotations embodied in reviews. For information address HarperCollins Publishers Ltd, Suite 2900, Hazelton Lanes, 55 Avenue Road, Toronto, Canada M5R 3L2.

http://www.harpercollins.com

First published in hardcover by Collins Publishers: 1987
First published in paperback by Collins Publishers: 1988
First HarperCollins Publishers Ltd paperback edition: 1990
Sixth printing: 1995
Revised paperback edition published by HarperCollins Publishers Ltd: 1996
Second printing: 1998

Canadian Cataloguing in Publication Data

Wilson, Eric
The Green Gables detectives

(A Liz Austen mystery)
ISBN 0-00-648157-4

I. Title. II. Series: Wilson, Eric. A Liz Austen mystery.

PS8595.I583G74 1996 jC813'.54 C95-933349-5
PZ7.W55Gr 1996

---

98 99 ❖ OPM 10 9 8 7 6 5 4 3 2

Printed and bound in the United States

cover design: Richard Bingham
cover and chapter illustrations: Richard Row
logo photograph: Lawrence McLagan

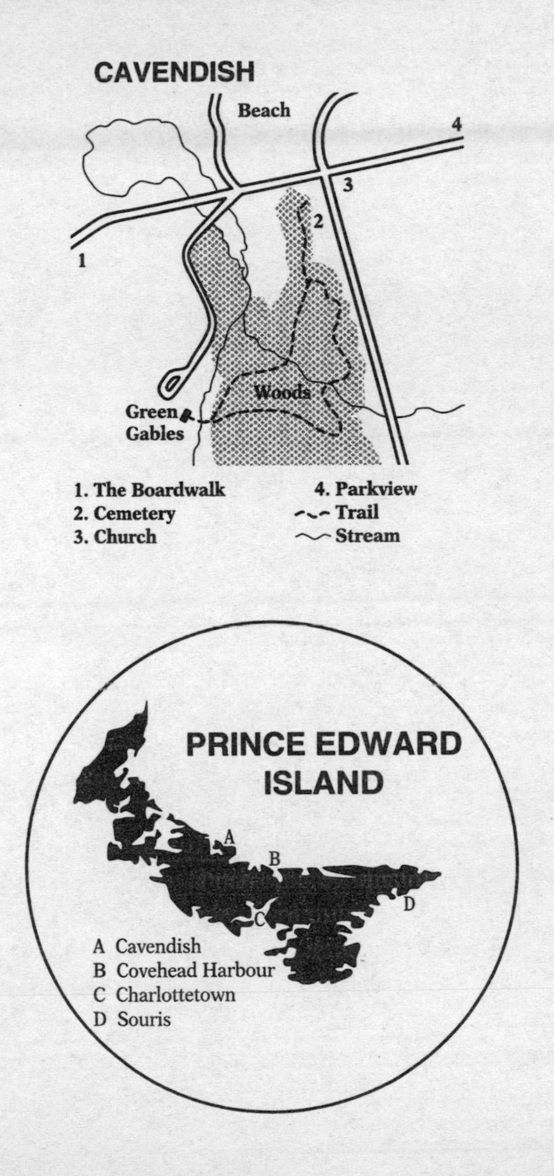
CAVENDISH
Beach
4
3
2
1
Woods
Green
Gables
1. The Boardwalk
2. Cemetery
3. Church
4. Parkview
Trail
Stream
PRINCE EDWARD
ISLAND
A
B
C
D
A Cavendish
B Covehead Harbour
C Charlottetown
D Souris

1

I stood by the tombstone, alone in the night.

Stars blinked through the trees around me. It had taken enormous courage to enter the cemetery but now I couldn't move. The tombstones were old, leaning crookedly, some shaped into crosses. Reaching out I touched cold marble, then gasped when a dark shape ran swiftly past and disappeared into the woods behind me.

"Relax," I whispered to myself. "It was only a farm cat. There's nothing to be afraid of."

Except the night, the graveyard, and spirits that prowl.

Managing a smile at my foolishness, I listened to the distant pounding of waves along the shoreline, then moved further into the cemetery. But again I stopped. The wind moaned in my ears as I stared at the dark tombstones, and a shiver went down my spine.

Then a hand touched me.

With a scream, I whirled around. Looking solemnly at me was a Japanese girl I'd met briefly an hour before. "So sorry," she whispered. "Please forgive such a scare."

I tried to smile. "Seen anything of our quarry?"

"Please?"

"Our quarry—you know, that woman."

"Ah yes." The girl stepped closer and I could see the excitement in her eyes. She was about my age and colouring but really beautiful, with a perfect complexion and thick black hair. "Perhaps she hides near grave of famous Maud."

"That's my theory, too. Trouble is, I'm too scared to go find out by myself."

"We try together. In this way we are strong, yes?"

"I guess so," I said, glancing around the cemetery. It was true I felt slightly braver now that I had company, but I still counted slowly to 10 for good luck. And as we started walking up the slope past the tombstones, I had to fight a terrible urge to look over my shoulder for lurking ghosts. But somehow I kept my eyes straight ahead until the girl touched my arm.

"Did you see? In shadows, light reflected from spectacles."

"You must be half cat," I whispered, "I can't see anything except . . ." Then my heart skipped a beat as just then I saw it too: a quick glimpse of twin circles of glass. Then nothing, just the darkness of shrubs beside a thick slab of marble. "She's hiding by that grave," I said in excitement. "We've done it! We're the first to find Marilla!"

All my fears evaporated as we rushed towards the grave and a figure stepped out of hiding. "Congratulations," she said, shaking our hands, "you're good detectives."

"This girl gets the credit," I said. "She spotted your glasses."

"Well done. What's your name?"

"Makiko Tanaka," the girl replied, smiling shyly.

"I'm Liz Austen," I said. "So far I love your Mystery Weekend!"

The woman smiled briefly. She looked about fifty, quite heavy, with greying hair pulled back in a severe bun. The old-fashioned spectacles did nothing for her face and she really didn't suit her gingham dress with its high collar, but of course she *was* pretending to be Marilla Cuthbert, one of the famous characters in *Anne of Green Gables*.

"What happens now?" I asked.

"I'll call the others to gather here, then explain."

Cupping her mouth, Marilla released a powerful bellow: "Everyone report to the graveyard!" As a couple of voices answered from the woods I looked at the tombstone where she'd been hiding. In the pale light of the stars I made out the name of Lucy Maud Montgomery and again felt the shiver of pleasure I'd experienced several days ago when I arrived on Prince Edward Island and first visited the grave of the woman who'd written the wonderful 'Anne books.'

Several dark figures emerged from the woods and started up the slope: a man with a meaty face and thick moustache, a couple of teenagers, an old man using a silver-headed cane, a woman with red hair and another wearing sandals, and some people who were such typical tourists that one even carried a camera even though it was night-time. As they approached, a fat man was puffing from the strain and a woman with a sour mouth was shaking her head.

"I didn't expect this! You should have warned us there'd be walking involved."

"And scares," the red-head said. "Searching the woods for your hiding place was a terrifying experience."

"I can't apologize," Marilla replied. "Mystery weekends are supposed to be scary." She adjusted her glasses, then looked at us all. "It was just an hour ago that I gave you those clues at Green Gables. Liz and Makiko found my hiding place but more puzzles lie ahead for everyone. If you would just . . ."

But at this moment she was interrupted by a man who'd arrived without warning. Marilla was clearly shocked when he reached her side and she first saw him. A hand flew to her mouth and I heard a gasp. As she struggled for words, the man smiled weakly.

"Sorry I'm late. Have I missed all the excitement? I was obviously given the wrong starting time."

"Excuses!" Marilla shook her head angrily. "You always were a great one for excuses." Turning away from him, she took a deep breath. "Now, where was I?"

"More challenges," said the young woman in sandals. "Something about a Captain?"

"Oh yes." Again Marilla paused for a deep breath. "From the time she was a young girl, Maud dreamed of being a writer. When she was fifteen her first poem was published." Taking a cigarette lighter from her pocket, she held it up as a signal. We followed her eyes towards the woods and, a few seconds later, saw two men emerge carrying lanterns and dressed as ancient seamen. "Maud's poem was about these men and what actually happened to them near this place. One is Captain Le Force, 'tall and dark and stern,' as she described him, and the other is the murderous mate, 'with vicious, brutal face.' "

The men stood facing each other. Then, by the lanterns' flickering light, I caught sight of the pistols they were carrying. A nerve throbbed in my throat.

"The men have come ashore from their ship, known as a privateer. They've quarreled about sharing their booty, and are about to settle the matter with a duel."

An eerie look came over Marilla's face as she began to recite the poem:

A look of craven fear was stamped
Upon the mate's low, brutal face,
Mingled with sinister cunning, as
Before the tent he took his place.

The captain, calm, composed and firm,
Betrayed no trace of doubt or fear;
His face still wore its cool contempt,
His lips, their cold, sardonic sneer.

"Twelve paces off, I'll stand," he said,
And, with his pistol in his hand,
He lightly turned upon his heel
And calmly walked toward his stand.

As Marilla spoke, the Captain and the Mate began to act out exactly what she was saying. Then, with the Captain's back turned, the mate raised his pistol and shot him! Stunned, I watched the captain fall in a crumpled heap.

"That can't have happened!"

"My dear girl," Marilla replied, "it *did* happen, just as you saw. Men are treacherous creatures."

"But we must do something! We've got to help the captain."

"Very well, help him."

With Makiko at my side, I raced down the slope past the tombstones. The mate, who had walked forward to stand over the captain's body, looked towards us. Then he scrambled over a fence and disappeared into the woods.

Reaching the captain, I knelt beside him. There was no blood, and his breathing was regular, but I was totally captured by the drama of the moment. As the others came closer I turned and said, "We've got to capture that creep!"

"Impossible," one of the teenagers said. "He could be hiding anywhere."

"I agree," said the fat man. "I've read Maud's poem, and she says the mate escaped. We can't change history."

The woman wearing the sandals shook her head. "You're wrong. We have a civic duty to help. I say we go into the woods, sticking close together for safety, and search for the mate." She looked at Marilla. "What do you think?"

For a moment she hesitated, then nodded. "It's a good plan."

"Then let's go!" Standing up, the young woman pointed at a white gate. "We can get into the woods through there."

I started forward, then noticed the old man was having trouble with his silver-headed cane, which kept sinking into the soft ground. "May I help you, sir?"

"Thank you." With a shy smile he took my arm. "Perhaps I shouldn't have signed up for such a strenuous event, but I love the Green Gables books. So far the Mystery Weekend is quite thrilling, wouldn't you say?"

"Absolutely." I managed a grin but inwardly I was choked because his heavy body made him walk so slowly. If we kept moving like a couple of snails through molasses we'd never have a chance of finding the mate.

But fortunately the others were waiting by the gate for us, and for the woman in sandals.

"One of them fell off," she said with a laugh. "I should have worn something more practical." Then she looked over my shoulder and her eyes widened. "Oh no! Look what's happened!"

Turning, I stared in disbelief at the captain's body. Jutting from his back was a dagger.

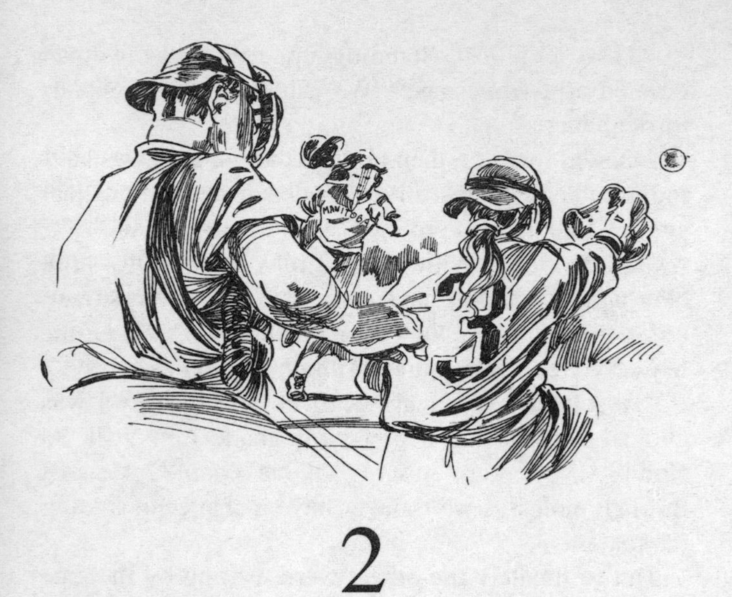

2

Quickly I started toward the captain but a strong hand grabbed my arm. Looking up, I saw it was the man with the chubby face.

"One minute please." He had a British accent. "I'm Inspector Lyall Cameron of Scotland Yard. I'm visiting Canada on my holidays, and it's fortunate that I happen to be here tonight. Stand back while I examine the body."

I couldn't help shivering as he knelt beside the captain to study the dagger. The lanterns cast a yellow glare that almost made the Inspector's face look evil, but I quickly shook off that idea—imagine not trusting Scotland Yard! Still, one of our apparently-innocent group must have stabbed the captain's body when nobody was watching.

Who? And why?

His face troubled, the Inspector stood up. "I must take statements from you all. Murder is a serious business."

Marilla held up her hand. "Now you all face a major challenge. One of you is secretly the person who stabbed Captain Le Force. Listen carefully as the Inspector takes each statement, then analyze all the evidence. You've got twenty-four hours to figure out the villain's identity, or the killer will strike again tomorrow night."

"That's when we meet at Green Gables?" I asked.

Marilla nodded. "We'll gather in the house where the story of *Anne of Green Gables* was set. Just remember—the killer will strike again, unless one of you has figured out the truth, can unmask the villain *and* give your reasons why."

As the Inspector began taking statements I listened carefully. More than anything in the world I wanted to be the one who discovered the villain's secret identity.

* * *

The next day I got into major trouble.

It started with someone throwing a hard object at me. Fortunately it was only a softball! Our team of 'Manitoba All-Stars' had been invited to PEI for an important tournament and today we were playing the island's own champs. A huge mob of their friends and parents had gathered at the Cavendish diamond to cheer them on, so my stomach was in knots as the umpire called *play ball!*

The Island pitcher delivered like a bazooka, and our batters went down swinging. Going to the pitcher's mound, I tried to calm my stomach. The first PEI batter was so tiny I didn't expect trouble but she immediately connected for a single. The fans went crazy, and I started to sweat.

The next batter had a weakness for inside pitches. She swung widely at two, then could only stare as I smoked my next pitch over the corner of the plate. Grinning, I waited for her to leave in disgrace but the umpire called, "Ball one!"

I stared at him in disbelief, then shook my head. As our coach yelled encouragement I let fly again but the batter creamed the pitch for a home run. The PEI girls danced around in jubilation as our coach walked slowly to the mound. "Tough luck, Liz. Feeling rattled?"

"You bet! I had that girl struck out, but the ump blew the call. He's prejudiced!"

"Don't be silly. Now calm down, and let's get back into the game."

I reached into my hip pocket to touch the good-luck charm my brother Tom had given me. It was a rabbit's foot joined to a four-leaf clover and it seemed to help because we kept PEI from scoring again as the game continued.

I was the lead-off batter in the fifth inning. Getting a signal from my coach I waited for the pitch and then shifted quickly to bunt. But the umpire screamed *batter's out!* before the ball even reached me.

I turned to him in shock. "What are you saying?"

Pulling off his mask, he stared at me. "You're out. O-U-T."

"But why?"

"You stepped out of the batter's box."

I look down at the red dirt. "There's no box here. The lines have gotten scuffed out since the game started."

"No matter. I know where they were."

"But I don't! That's not fair!"

He crossed his arms. They were muscular and hairy in his short-sleeved shirt, and his face also had the muscular look of someone who knows he's got all the power. "I'm the ump, and I say you're out. No back-talk now, or I'll throw you out of the game."

Muttering under my breath, I returned to the bench and watched glumly as our team went down swinging. Taking the field, we kept PEI from scoring again but we remained behind 2-1 as the game continued.

Then it happened.

I was on second base, watching a hit sail towards the outfield. The moment the ball was caught I took off, hoping to reach home plate and tie the score. As the crowd screamed, I accelerated, then slid into the plate. My foot touched it, then I felt the catcher tag me.

"*Yer outta there!*" cried the ump.

Rolling over in the dirt, I stared at him. "You're kidding! I beat the throw!"

"I repeat: you're out."

Jumping up, I smacked red dust off my uniform while I fought down my anger. Then with a shaking voice I said, "Mr Ump, you're wrong. *Wrong, wrong, wrong*. I beat that throw!"

Slowly he removed his mask. His face was seamed like leather and his beady little eyes were unfriendly. "I've met some snollygosters in my time, miss, but you take the cake. You're kicked out of this game."

"What?"

"You heard me. Go ride the bench."

Turning toward my coach, I raised my hands in a gesture of amazement and dismay. I returned to the bench, choking back tears of disappointment. When our team took the field I was left alone, until a boy suddenly appeared beside me and said, "Hi there." He was tall and good-looking, with dark hair and hazel eyes, and seemed about my age. "Mind if I sit down?"

"Be my guest." I shifted over, wishing I wasn't covered with dirt from sliding into home plate.

"Too bad you were kicked out," the boy said.

I shrugged. "That's life."

"My name's Aaron Johnson. You're a good player, Liz."

"How'd you know my name?"

"I asked the scorekeeper."

Feeling better, I cheered loudly for our team. Then I stared at the ump. "They must have found that guy at the CNIB."

"What's that?"

"The Canadian National Institute for the Blind."

Aaron laughed. "He's just a volunteer ump."

"He called me a snollygoster. What's that mean?"

Aaron shrugged. "I've never asked him. Anyway Liz, it's only a game."

"Tell that to the folks back home. They're expecting glittering trophies and first-place golds."

"Really?"

"I guess not, but my brother's going to give me a rough time. My only hope is to solve the Green Gables Mystery Weekend."

He looked surprised. “You’re into that?”

“Sure.” I described last night’s events, and the challenge we’d been given by Marilla. “It’s really neat, Aaron. You should get involved, especially since you live on the island.”

“I *am* involved.”

“What do you mean?”

“I’ll tell you another time.”

Standing up, Aaron walked away. I watched him join some other boys in the crowd, then returned my concentration to the game. Manitoba managed to get players on base in the final inning but they were left stranded as PEI took the victory. We gave them a cheer, went over to shake hands, then stood around staring into space. It was hard to believe we’d flown halfway across the country only to lose.

My coach put an arm around my shoulders. “Don’t be blue, Liz. You played a good game.”

“Thanks, Coach.”

I smiled at her. A really cheerful person, Sandra was a long-distance runner and a great softball player who’d put her heart into this team. We’d had some long and tough practices after arriving in PEI, and had managed to win our opening games against New Brunswick and a team from Maine, but now we were finished and PEI would play in the final. I felt depressed, but Sandra’s dark eyes still had their sparkle.

“Wait till next year, eh?”

“I guess so.”

“That was . . . well, at last!”

She looked across the diamond at a young woman who was approaching with a man who looked about forty-five. The woman was smiling, but her hands were up in self-defence. "Don't say anything, Sis! I'm sorry we're late, but Humphrey's not a softball fan."

"No matter." Sandra turned to me. "I'm pleased you can meet my sister Katie. She's from Winnipeg too, but she's living here for the summer."

"In Cavendish?"

Katie shook her head. "I'm in Charlottetown. Have you heard of the Festival there? Every summer they perform a musical version of *Anne of Green Gables* and I have the role of Anne's best friend, Diana Barry."

"You look perfect for the part, Katie." This was true: she had a big smile and lovely dark eyes that sparkled like her sister's but I thought she was a bit too old for the part. "You're not a teenager, are you?"

"No, I'm twenty-two, but it's amazing what they can do with professional make-up."

The man beside her smiled. "I could use s-s-some . . ." He paused, trying not to stutter, then tried again. "I could use s-s-some of that make-up."

"I'm sorry, Humphrey, I haven't introduced you."

As names were exchanged I studied the man's face. His green eyes were really nice but the thick glasses he wore made them difficult to see. Although his eyebrows were really bushy, he'd lost most of his brown hair. And besides being pretty fat, he'd actually worn a necktie to a softball game! For a minute, I was kind of wondering about Katie's taste in men, but if she was as nice as her sister then I figured he must be okay, too.

And then I noticed that the twinkle in Sandra's eyes had been replaced by something soft and feminine, and there was something different in her voice as she asked Humphrey questions about his work.

"I'm a s-s-stagehand at the Festival, Miss Michie, and . . ."

"Please, call me Sandra."

"You're very kind. I work behind the s-s-scenes at the musical, moving furniture and props. I wonder if, no, probably not . . ." His voice trailed off and he stared at the ground, rubbing the back of his neck. For a moment there was an awkward silence, then Sandra looked at him hopefully.

"Yes?"

"I, well . . . I s-s-suppose you wouldn't care to s-s-see the musical from backstage? I could make arrangements."

"Why, Humphrey, I'd love to."

"It would be a chance to watch your s-s-sister as Diana Barry. What a s-s-super s-s-star in the making."

Katie laughed. "Humphrey's a charmer."

"Oh, I'm sure he's right," Sandra said. "I remember when you were a little girl, performing 'shows' in our living room. Mom and Pop always said you'd end up on Broadway." She turned to Humphrey. "Being an older sister, I spoiled her rotten when she was young."

He smiled affectionately at Katie. "I don't blame you."

"Gosh, Sandra!" I said. "How lucky can you get! Try to remember everything so you can tell me all about it."

Humphrey nodded. "Well . . . there just might be room for both of you . . . I'll make the arrangements."

"That would be wonderful," I said, giving him a hug. Humphrey wasn't the world's most gorgeous man but he certainly seemed nice, and I couldn't blame

Sandra for showing some interest. After all, a Great Romance might result: and if it did, I'd have watched it from the start!

As I said goodbye I wondered if Katie had planned this all along, then watched until they'd walked to Humphrey's dirty old car and lurched away in a cloud of blue exhaust. After that I remembered I had to get my stuff off the team bench. While I was collecting my things, I saw a man approaching. His face was familiar but it took a moment to remember he was last night's late arrival at the cemetery. Today in the sunshine I could see his face properly. He was about fifty, and quite nice looking with a neatly trimmed beard, pale blue eyes and a strong chin.

"So you're from Manitoba," he said. "Me too, and I think I recognized your coach. Isn't her name Sandra Michie?"

I made a motion with my head that could have been yes or no. I didn't want to give a total stranger information about my coach, so I was glad when he abruptly turned and walked away. He was shaking his head, probably thinking I was a nerd, but I couldn't help that.

Maybe he was perfectly harmless but you never know, and I wasn't about to wait around and find out. Besides, Marilla sure hadn't been too happy to see him last night.

3

That afternoon I went back to the cemetery.

Determined to unmask the villain, I was hoping to find clues at the scene of the crime. A hot sun burned down as I passed under the entrance arch that read *Resting place of L.M. Montgomery* and looked at all the tombstones. It was strange how they'd scared me last night and now I just felt peaceful as I wandered past the old marble mottled with orange moss, noticing how some memorials used nice wording like 'Fell asleep,' some showed Bibles and one had the hands of a man and woman shaking goodbye.

I took a picture of Maud's grave, then left some wild flowers I'd picked. As I wandered down the slope towards the place where the Captain had been lying I saw someone kneeling on the grass, carefully examining the ground. As I came closer, she looked up and I saw it was Makiko, the Japanese girl I'd met last night.

"Hi there," I said cheerfully. "Checking for clues?"

"Good day, Austen-san. Have you good fortune in baseball?"

"No," I said, surprised. "How'd you know about my team?"

Those beautiful black eyes lit up. "I love baseball, therefore I follow tournament most closely. I miss today's game only because of detective work." She pointed at the ground. "See here. Do you have theory?"

Kneeling down, I examined the ground. Nearby were the holes made when the old man's cane sank into the soft soil, but I couldn't see anything else until my face was practically touching the ground. "You mean those little marks?"

"Yes."

"I should have brought a magnifying glass." Carefully I studied them. "There's 10. Do you think someone's fingers made the marks?"

"Not fingers, but toes I believe." She pointed to a couple of bigger indentations. "Look there."

"Knees! Someone knelt beside the Captain to stab him with that dagger. But nobody last night was barefooted, except . . ." I snapped my fingers. "Except the woman in sandals! Her toes were bare."

Makiko grinned. "We are hot-shot detectives, yes?"

"I can't wait until tonight! Let's nail that woman as soon as we arrive at Green Gables and claim first prize."

"Caution, Austen-san. You have examined rules? If wrong person is named, we are . . . how you say?"

"You're right, Makiko. If we're wrong, and she's not

the villain, we're disqualified and can't pick anyone else. But let's watch her really closely." I stood up. "Do you live on the island?"

"No, no. My home is Japan. My father travels to beautiful Prince Edward Island on business and I beg him, please, take me to country of red-haired Anne. How much I love story of orphanage sending her in mistake to Matthew and Marilla who want boy but grow to love Anne."

"So you've read the story?"

"Oh yes." She opened her canvas shoulderbag. "Look, here is book."

"Wow, it's in Japanese."

"We study story in school. Each summer many Japanese visit island for seeing Green Gables. In Japan we have Buttercups, fan society for Lucy Maud Montgomery. Much study of her life." She took out another book. "Please to read."

I laughed. "I'd love to, but my Japanese is a little rusty. These look like pictures of PEI, but what do the words say?"

"Is guide book to island, telling of author's birthplace and where she was teacher. Is most wonderful to be here, Austen-san!"

"That's great, but I wish you'd call me Liz."

"No, no." She shook her head vigorously. "Is very rude."

"Okay, but what does *san* mean?"

"It gives you honour."

"That's really nice. Is it okay to call you Makiko?"

"Oh yes. Is custom of Canada."

"Why do you speak my language so well?"

"Thank you for saying this. I study at American School in my city of Kyoto. So too my sister. Is desire of parents for knowledge of languages."

"So you can get better jobs when you're finished university?"

"Perhaps." She smiled. "Or perhaps for me is home and family. This very happy thought, yes?"

I nodded, then stared into space for a moment thinking about my own future. Marriage, kids, a career? Anything was possible, which felt nice.

Makiko pointed at an old shack beside the fence. "Austen-san, we must investigate. Perhaps is lurking place for killer."

"I think you mean hiding place, Makiko, but you're right. Let's go see if it means anything."

Unfortunately, the shack didn't provide any useful information. There was a rusty old lock on the door and the window had been painted over, so it was impossible to see inside. "Maybe it was used to store a lawn mower and gardening stuff," I suggested, "but these days the workers probably come in a truck from the city with their equipment."

Kneeling down, I studied the door handle. "Nobody's been inside this place for a while."

"How so?"

"Look at the dust. It wouldn't be here if someone had touched the handle recently."

"Ah!" Makiko nodded her head. "Excellent idea."

At that moment a shadow fell across the door. Looking up, I saw that we were being watched by a woman who'd approached without making a sound. The lines around her eyes were grim and her mouth was turned down at the corners, so I didn't have any trouble recognizing her from the night before. She was the woman who'd organized the Mystery Weekend and played the role of Marilla.

"What are you girls doing?"

"Looking for clues. We're going to be the winners for sure! Makiko's a fabulous detective—she's already figured out that . . ."

"Please Austen-san, do not shame my idea until more evidence known."

"You're right, Makiko. Me and my big mouth."

The woman crossed her arms over her heavy body. She wasn't wearing the gingham dress or the old-fashioned spectacles today, but her hair was still in a bun and she was wearing drab colours that made her look dowdy. At school I'd studied colour combinations and was about to suggest a red blouse or a forest-green skirt but I decided to keep my mouth shut. Somehow I knew my advice wouldn't be appreciated, and it would be rude to criticize someone I'd just met.

"Well girls, I'm impressed by your enthusiasm. Perhaps you'll tell all your friends about my Mystery Weekend and I'll make some real money out of this venture."

"The tickets are pretty expensive," I said. "It cost me all my babysitting money."

"You won't regret it."

"Is your real name Marilla?"

"Of course not. You may call me Miss Martin. I play the role of Marilla in the musical *Anne of Green Gables*. I've been with the Festival for years but acting is no way to get rich. When I heard about people organizing mystery weekends at famous places like Niagara Falls, I figured the idea would work at Green Gables too."

"Were some of the people in the cemetery last night actors?"

Miss Martin nodded. "Captain Le Force and the mate were both actors, and so were a few others. Your challenge is to decide, from the clues, which person is secretly acting the part of a killer."

"I just met the girl who's Diana in the musical. She was really nice."

"She'll be at Green Gables tonight, playing the role of Diana. The actress who's Anne in the show will also be there."

"But what about the play?"

"It's only performed some nights of the week. Tonight there's a different show at the Festival with other actors." Miss Martin sighed. "I'm taking a big risk producing this Mystery Weekend, but I think it's going to work. Would you like to walk through the woods to Green Gables? I'm going to check a few details at the house before this evening's events."

"Sure thing! Our team's had so many practices and games that I haven't had a chance to visit Green Gables yet." I winked at Makiko. "Besides which, maybe we can get some inside information to help unmask the killer."

Miss Martin shook her head. "That is highly unlikely. Do you think I'd give away my secrets? It took a lot of work to plan this weekend and I'm determined it'll only be solved by careful sleuthing, not cheating."

What a touchy woman! I was tempted to forget the walk, but then I relaxed and followed her to a trail into the woods. From what I'd read about L.M. Montgomery I knew she'd lived near here as a girl, and followed this very route when she visited her relatives at

Green Gables. It was a strange experience to actually be following in her footsteps. Spruce and maple and birch trees grew all along the trail as it wandered past rotting logs and thick undergrowth. Our approach startled a robin, which flew away through the splotches of sunlight filtering through the leaves, while a number of other birds twirped and darted among the branches.

Makiko touched my arm. "Often since coming to island I have searched for the White Lady, famous birch tree in writings of famous Maud. Also I look for signs of her school, but nothing remains. So sad."

Miss Martin pointed at a bench in a sunny glade.

"That's where the school used to be. Let's rest for a minute. My feet are killing me."

I was too full of energy to sit down, so I paced back and forth along the red path while Miss Martin fanned her face. "Is it true the ground here is rusty and that's why it's red?"

"That's correct. There's iron in the soil."

I looked at the carpet of green ferns and the moss hanging from trees. "This is such a lovely place. I wonder if Maud dreamed of being an author when she was a girl going to school here."

"No doubt she did, but Maud only became a successful author through hard work and sheer determination. I intend to follow her example and make my Mystery Weekend a great success." For a moment Miss Martin was silent, watching a blue jay hop from branch to branch. "People think Maud made it big from the start, but that's not true. She practised her writing for years while she taught school, and looked after her grandparents at their farm house. It took her eighteen months to write *Anne of Green Gables* and then years to find a publisher."

"How come? That book has sold millions."

"You're right, and it's been translated into thirty-four different languages. But nobody wanted the manuscript at first, so Maud shoved it into an old hatbox and forgot about it. Years later she decided to try again and sent it to a Boston publisher. A woman from PEI was working for the company and she kept nagging them until Maud was offered a contract."

"And the rest is history! What a wonderful life she had."

"I don't agree." Miss Martin stood up, brushing twigs from her skirt. "Certainly she had many successes, but she also had problems with her grandparents and then later with her husband. Life can be difficult, young lady, especially where men are concerned, so be warned. They're nothing but trouble."

"My Dad's great, and Mom really loves him."

"Then she's one of the lucky ones. I was in love once but he dropped me cold without a word of warning. I've never forgotten."

"Why didn't you try again with someone else?"

"Once bitten, twice shy." Above Miss Martin's head a crow made a rasping cry and then rose into the air. She looked up absently and didn't say anything for a minute or two. "But after all these years he's just turned up again. Isn't that strange?"

I was dying to ask some questions but I could tell Miss Martin was an obstinate type so I kept silent as we continued along to a small bridge over a stream. I gazed down at the pebbles on the rusty bed of the stream and listened to the water swirling around rocks and dead branches, then looked at Makiko.

"I bet this is the place where Anne and Diana swore an oath to be kindred spirits."

"Was it not on path near Diana's home?"

"Maybe you're right. Boy, you know the story inside-out!"

Makiko smiled. "Gracious thanks, Austen-san. Perhaps one day we shall be kindred spirits like Anne and Diana."

"Want to know something? Our combined brain-power is going to blow this Mystery Weekend wide open. We can't fail!"

"Sincerely I hope for this."

A twig snapped somewhere along the path, then I saw a young couple approaching. The woman was a bit much with her blond hair piled high in fancy curls and flashy jewellery all over her hands and throat and ears, but the guy was fabulous. His dark hair spilled over his forehead, his jacket collar was turned up over a red-striped shirt, and he was tall with a slim, athletic body. As I feasted my eyes I realized Miss Martin was also staring, but only because she was furious.

"I can't believe it! You are deliberately ignoring my instructions."

"Aw, come on." He raised his beautiful shoulders in a shrug. "It's a great day to be outdoors. Why hide at home?"

"Because I'm paying you to act in my Mystery Weekend, and part of your job is to remain in hiding today. What if you're spotted by one of the guests and it helps them to solve the mystery?"

The sound of his laughter was wonderful. "Everyone's at the beach. Nobody'll see me."

"What about these girls? They're guests."

Again the shrug, then he smiled at me. "Hi there. I'm A.P. Cole and this is my friend, Jeni. Having a nice day?"

"I'm, uh, yes, I mean . . ."

Miss Martin interrupted my feeble stuttering by stepping in front of him. "Listen to me. Go home this minute."

"I don't want to."

"Then you'll never act in another Mystery Weekend."

He leaned forward to kiss her cheek. "You don't mean that."

"Your charm won't work on me. Go home immediately."

Smiling, he reached for Jeni's hand and they strolled away. I shook my head, wondering what he saw in that woman with her bleached-blond hair and all the jewellery, then turned to Makiko. "Isn't he *great*? Isn't he the most perfect specimen of humanity you ever saw walking the face of the earth?"

"Is not my type Austen-san, but I have theory. This actor was last night the cruel mate, yes?"

"I think you're right. Maybe . . ."

But again I was interrupted by Miss Martin. "You mustn't discuss this! Please, pretend you didn't see him."

For a moment I was annoyed, but then I realized she was only upset about her carefully planned Mystery Weekend being spoiled. "We won't mention A.P. Cole again Miss Martin, but you know something? Your weekend is a fabulous idea and it'll be a huge success."

The lines around her mouth softened into a brief smile, but she jumped when another twig snapped. I hoped that A.P. Cole had returned but it was only a woman loaded down with camera equipment. After watching her shoot the bridge from some fancy angles we continued along the path until there was a loud burst of applause from somewhere in the trees.

"What happens?" Makiko asked.

"Don't worry," Miss Martin said. "It's only a tour."

"Please?"

"These woods, and Green Gables itself, are part of a national park run by the government. Guides take tourists on walks to see famous places like Lovers' Lane. When the walk ends the people applaud their guide."

A mob of people came toward us along the path, laughing and chatting about their tour. I stood to one side as they passed, then looked at Miss Martin. "Don't Maud's relatives live at Green Gables?"

"Not any more. As a little girl she came through these woods to Green Gables to visit the elderly cousins who inspired the characters of Matthew and Marilla. Years later the house and its woods and fields were purchased by the government for the public to visit." She paused, thinking. "Do you know, more than a hundred thousand people visit Green Gables every year? What a potential gold mine for my Mystery Weekends!"

As we crossed a footbridge and left the woods I looked up a steep slope, then stopped to stare. At last! Standing at the top of the hill, shining in the sun, was Green Gables. "Wow! It's way more beautiful than I expected. Look at all those flowers and trees, and the sunshine sparkling off the windows." I turned to Makiko. "It's like I'm actually Maud, coming to visit her cousins."

"Is time for picture."

I stood on the footbridge, grinning into Makiko's camera as the shutter clicked, then Miss Martin broke the mood. "Come along, girls, let's get moving." As she started up the slope, grumbling with the effort, I snapped a quick shot and studied the house as Makiko and I climbed toward it, passing Miss Martin on the way.

"I've never exactly known what a gable is, but it must be that upper part of the wall that's painted green."

Makiko grinned. "Good thinking, Austen-san. Very good."

"Hey! That sounds like sarcasm to me."

She laughed. "Please to forgive."

"Okay, but only if you'll take one more picture of me." Sitting on some stone steps built into the hillside, I leaned toward a flower bed to sniff a huge mass of blossoms, then looked at Miss Martin as she came puffing up the hill.

"Would you be in the picture with me?"

"What a kind thought."

Makiko raised her camera and captured the pair of us together on the steps, then I suggested asking a tourist to photograph us all together but Makiko shook her head.

"No, no. Very bad luck. Three people in picture brings terrible misfortune. Even such thought fills me with dread."

She looked so frightened that a chill ran up my spine. Maybe it's because I'm a wee bit superstitious myself but her fear was so strong that I was sorry I'd suggested the photograph. Then I shook off my feelings and turned to Miss Martin with a smile.

"Thanks for bringing us here. I can't wait to see inside Green Gables."

"Well, you're not going to." Standing up, she took a deep gulp of air. "I absolutely forbid it."

"What do you mean?"

"It'll spoil all my plans for tonight. You'll simply have to wait."

"But I want to see Anne's room and everything *now*."

"What rubbish. You children today are so spoiled. When I was a girl we obeyed our elders, and we didn't question what they said."

With another sigh she continued on to the house and disappeared through the door. There was no law keeping me from going inside but I didn't want to upset Miss Martin further so instead I checked out a nearby gift shop with Makiko, and then chatted with a friendly guide wearing a Parks Canada uniform. She told us about people coming here from Japan on their honeymoon and how some brides break down sobbing when they first see Green Gables.

"Is true," Makiko said. "Is same experience of my cousin. On her living room wall, to this day, is special certificate presented by Island government on arrival for honeymoon. Is treasured possession."

"That's wonderful," the guide said. "It makes me proud to be an Islander." She glanced at her watch. "I've got another tour, but why don't you watch the old-fashioned games? They're starting now."

She pointed across the lawn to a group of young kids and their parents being gathered together by a teenage girl dressed in a full skirt with an apron, and a boy wearing knickerbocker trousers and suspenders over a striped shirt.

"Hey, that's Aaron."

"Who please?" asked Makiko.

"He's a local guy I met at the baseball game this morning. Let's go say hello."

As we crossed the lawn Aaron looked my way and waved, then concentrated his attention on giving the kids their instructions. We sat down to watch as five of them tried to roll huge hoops across the lawn, pushing them with sticks. Then Aaron and the girl organized wheelbarrow and sack races, followed by a three-legged race. This one provided the only drama when a pair of girls tripped just before the finish line and two boys took the victory. As one girl burst into tears her mother rushed forward with comforting arms and her father came right behind with his video camera, shouting *keep crying!* as he zoomed in on the girl's tears.

"What a video freak. You guys should never have invented those things."

Makiko laughed. "What of telephone, created in Canada? I and friends are freaks for it."

"I guess you're right," I said, standing up. "Let's say hi to Aaron."

When I introduced them Aaron removed his cloth cap and bowed low to Makiko. "Welcome to the island. Enjoying your honeymoon?"

She giggled and Aaron smiled at me. "Care for some homemade ice cream? I bet it's the best you've ever tasted." Taking both of us by the arm, he led the way across the lawn to a bench outside the house, where a teenager was turning the crank of an antique machine. "There's whipping cream and eggs and brown sugar in there."

"Remember Anne," I said to Makiko, "and how she'd never tasted ice cream?"

Aaron was right: this stuff was the best ever, smooth and cold and delicious. As the icy heaven slid down my throat I leaned down beside a little red-haired girl watching gravely as her ice cream was dished out. "How old are you?"

"Three."

Her grandmother winked at me. "Colleen's actually two, but she wants everyone to think she's older."

"What an adorable little girl. I should get her picture—she's a perfect little Anne of Green Gables."

"Don't say that! She's getting tired of hearing it, and she's telling everyone so."

As I ate more ice cream I looked across the woods at the white spire of a distant church. "Isn't that beautiful?"

"Maud taught Sunday School there for years," Aaron said. "Tomorrow night there's a special memorial service for her, and afterwards there's refreshments in the church basement. I'm singing in the choir, so why don't you both come?"

"What a nice idea," I said feeling a flutter of pleasure in my tummy. "I'm billeted at a farm near the church, so I'll be there for sure."

"A couple of players from Moncton are staying at my place. Everyone in the area was asked to help out because so many teams are here." He gestured toward Green Gables. "By the way, how's the search for clues?"

"Not bad. We found some interesting stuff in the cemetery, then Miss Martin came along and invited us to walk over here."

Aaron looked alarmed. "She's at Green Gables?"

"Yes. She went inside just before we came over to watch you. Why, what's wrong?"

"Nothing." Aaron put on his cap. "Look, I'm really busy but maybe I'll see you another time." He walked quickly away, leaving me with an open mouth.

"What a rude thing to do! Have we got halitosis or something?"

"Please?"

"You know, bad breath." When she still looked blank I shook my head. "It's not important, but I can't understand why Aaron walked out on us. Maybe Miss Martin is right about men being nothing but trouble."

"Aaron nice person. Not trouble."

"I hope you're right." Feeling bothered by Aaron's strange behaviour, I wandered around with Makiko looking at the flower beds and listening to the wind sweep through the tall trees. Behind the house we found a well and I suggested it would be a good hiding place for a killer, or a dead body, if a murder happened during the evening.

"Murder?" Makiko looked doubtful. "Not in such pretty place."

"But we're on the trail of a murderer. Tonight could be really creepy."

4

The sunset was spectacular that evening. The huge, red circle slid into the sea while a layer of pink clouds spread across the horizon. After I'd left the farm a quarter-moon rose, throwing shadows everywhere in the cemetery. I kept hearing strange noises in the woods, so I was glad when I'd reached the footbridge and could see Green Gables at the top of the hill.

Then something terrible happened.

For just a second I saw silver flash low across the horizon. A shooting star! Quickly I repeated *money money money,* hoping to turn the omen into good fortune, but my heart was thudding as I approached the house because I was certain the shooting star meant death for someone.

Miss Martin was waiting outside the front door,

again wearing her old-fashioned clothes. I tried to produce a cheerful hello, then crossed all my fingers as I looked up at the sky. The omen had destroyed my good mood, but things improved when a car approached along a sideroad and Makiko stepped out.

"Austen-san," she called, "please to meet honoured father."

He had a friendly smile, gold-rimmed glasses and black hair with flecks of grey. We exchanged shy greetings, then he drove off and I turned to Makiko. Her eyes were so bright with excitement that I didn't have the heart to tell her about the shooting star. Instead I described the sunset as we walked toward the house.

"Tonight, Austen-san, we are detective champions, yes?"

"You bet! But let's be careful so we're not disqualified for a foolish guess."

As we reached the front three young people came outside to join Miss Martin. Right away I recognized Katie, all dressed up for her role as Diana Barry with ribbons in her pigtails, a checked apron over a white dress and high-button boots. Beside her was a girl who could only be Anne of Green Gables, but to me the best thing was seeing Aaron, even though I was still a bit annoyed at the way he'd suddenly walked off this afternoon. As I started to say hello, Miss Martin held up a hand.

"Young ladies, I want you to meet Anne, Diana and their friend Gilbert Blythe."

"Welcome to Green Gables," Anne said. "Come inside for some tea."

Makiko giggled. "What of raspberry cordial?"

"Marilla won't let me repeat that mistake!"

She gave Miss Martin a smile but it was lost on the woman, whose eyes were grim. Then headlights swept across her face as a car pulled to a stop. I expected to see another guest arriving but instead was surprised to recognize the man who'd umpired my softball game. As my skin prickled, I watched him approach carrying a sign that read STOP EXPLOITING GREEN GABLES!

"What's going on?" I whispered, stepping close to Aaron.

"Some of the locals are unhappy with Miss Martin for getting permission to use the house for her Mystery Weekend. They're calling it too commercial."

"He's not being fair," I said, staring at the ump. "Miss Martin's just trying to make a success of her life. And she's not hurting anyone."

As the ump began marching back and forth with the sign, Aaron stepped back into the shadows. "Last year he started a museum that's all about L.M. Montgomery," he whispered, "so I guess he's bothered by this new competition for tourist dollars. He probably thinks that if anyone is going to profit, it should be the Islanders."

"What a total bozo. First he throws me out of the game, now he wants to destroy Miss Martin's Mystery Weekend. He should be run off the island."

I guess my voice was kind of loud, because the ump gave me a dirty look as he continued parading. Aaron was about to say something when the front door opened and several people came out to see what was happening. I recognized 'Cameron of the Yard,' the old man with the fat body and silver-headed cane who had slowed me down so much the other night, the red-headed woman and several others, but one new face was a young priest in a black suit and faded collar. Although his appearance had been changed by make-up I was convinced I recognized him, and couldn't wait to discuss my theory with Makiko. But as I moved closer to her Miss Martin grabbed my arm and pushed me toward the door.

"Everyone go inside. We'll ignore this foolish man."

Waiting in the hallway was a man wearing overalls and a checked shirt with a corncob pipe in his mouth.

"I bet you're Matthew," I said, shaking his hand.

The floor creaked as I went into the parlour. An oil lamp cast a yellow glow over the red-headed woman, who sat on a black-satin sofa. The woman who had been wearing sandals last night was standing beside her and when I looked down, she was still wearing them! I couldn't believe it. They were looking at a thick family Bible, which I glanced at as I passed by to examine a frame on the wall.

"Know what this is, Makiko? A family wreath. People used to cut locks of hair from all the family, then weave them together to be framed."

"Most different."

"Know something really different? They also made funeral wreaths out of a dead person's hair."

She shivered. "Please, not to speak of funeral."

"You're right—sorry."

We went into the dining room, where a mantel clock ticked and a big maple table was set for tea. On the wall was the actual picture of children being blessed that was described in Maud's book but there was nothing else to remind me of the story, so I decided to find

Anne's room. As we went toward the stairs in the hallway I noticed Miss Martin speaking quietly to Matthew, then the front door opened and I saw the man who'd spoken to me after the softball game. His pale blue eyes glanced my way, then he saw Miss Martin and almost seemed to wince. With a brief nod to her he headed into the parlour.

"What nerve," Miss Martin sniffed. Seeing me, she pointed to the parlour. "In there. I'm going to explain what happens next." She whispered something to Matthew, then clapped her hands at some guests in the kitchen. "Come along now! Let's get moving."

The parlour was crowded with people but Makiko and I found a spot near the dining room entrance. "I'm sure that priest is secretly A.P. Cole. I'd know those gorgeous eyes anywhere."

"Is true, Austen-san. Could be secretly killer?"

"Maybe, but I still suspect that woman in the sandals. See how dirty her toenails are? I bet they got that way kneeling beside the captain's body last night." As Aaron came through the dining room I smiled. "Okay, I'm demanding a confession. Why'd you run away from us this afternoon?"

"Sorry about that. When Miss Martin hired me to play Gilbert she gave strict orders not to leave home today. But every Saturday I help with the kids' races so I came over anyway, hoping she wouldn't find out."

"No wonder you freaked when I said she was inside Green Gables. Are you in the musical at the Festival too?"

Aaron shook his head. "I got hired for this because the guy from the play couldn't be here tonight."

Miss Martin clapped her hands. "Quiet everyone. Pay attention. In a moment I'll hand out slips of paper. Some are clues to help your search for the killer, but others can trick you. The villain's goal is to kill each one of you before he or she can be unmasked, so some of you may die tonight!" She gave a strange giggle, then turned to Matthew. "My assistant will now pass out the clues, but please remember: among you is someone whose heart is filled with murder. *Who can that person be?*"

As Matthew handed out clues some guests looked puzzled by what they read while others rushed off immediately to investigate. I was on pins and needles as a single clue was given to Makiko and me and she read it aloud:

> "Find something black that once did shatter
> Over GB's head with quite a clatter;
> Upon the frame you'll find the name
> Of someone with a clue to claim."

For a minute we stared at each other, then I snapped my fingers. "GB must be Gilbert Blythe."

"Exact truth! And black is slate smashed upon head of Gilbert by red-haired Anne."

"Good work, but where do we find the slate? Anne and Gilbert wrote on them in class, but there's no schoolhouse around here." As I paused to think I tried not to worry that the other guests might already be closing in on the killer. "The slate's got to be in this house, but where?"

"Perhaps in bedroom of Anne?"

"You genius!"

Together we raced up the narrow stairs. Some guests were searching other rooms but no one was in Anne's, which had a brass bed with fluffy pillows and a white quilt. On a hook hung the pretty dress she'd been given by Matthew, and I also noticed a collection of seashells on the windowsill, but my eyes were really only searching for the slate. Then I spotted it, leaning against the wall beside Anne's carpetbag from the orphanage. Racing over, I grabbed the slate and immediately found a name taped to the frame.

"It's Matthew! But what do we do now?"

Makiko repeated part of the clue: "Upon the frame you'll find the name of someone with a clue to claim."

"Then let's find Matthew."

He was in a rocking chair in the kitchen, one foot resting on a large butter churn, smiling gently as he watched the red-headed woman exploring an old stove. She glanced at us suspiciously, perhaps thinking we were about to steal her clue, then relaxed when we raced over to Matthew.

"Your name's upon the frame," I whispered, "so what's the clue that we should claim?"

Slowly he removed his corncob pipe and used the stem to scratch his thin hair as he said:

> "Up those narrow stairs go once again
> Find somewhere dark where there's never rain;
> Around the walls search out a clue
> But careful! Splinters also wait for you."

Makiko and I exchanged puzzled looks, then she said, "Best to explore up the stairs? Perhaps answer then clear."

We left the kitchen, squeezed past two people examining an old typewriter in the narrow hallway, and had just started up the stairs when the pale-eyed man appeared above us. "It's bad luck to pass on the stairs," I said to Makiko, pulling her back to the hallway. The man studied us both as he came down, then we raced up. I led the way into a bedroom with scatter rugs on the hardwood floor and an overpowering floral wallpaper, but we couldn't see anything that helped make sense of Matthew's clue.

"What about the bureau?" I examined the design carved into the wood surrounding a mirror. "Could you get splinters from this thing?"

"Perhaps, but Matthew speak of somewhere dark. In this room light comes through windows in days."

"You're right, and the other rooms also have windows. The only place that's always dark is a closet, but these old houses didn't have them."

"So where keep clothes?"

"People hung them from hooks on the walls." I studied a large china pitcher and bowl. "In the old days you had to bring water to your bedroom in a pitcher, then wash in a bowl like this. It must have been a real nuisance, but I guess . . . Hey!"

"What is wrong?"

"Some houses had wardrobes!"

"Please?"

"People kept their clothes in wardrobes. They were pieces of furniture just like closets, and they were made of wood. Always dark *and* splinters!"

"Austen-san, you are hot-shot detective."

I grinned. "Thanks Makiko, but we've still got a problem. There's no wardrobe in this room."

We checked Anne's room without success, then went down the hallway. The old man with the silver-headed cane was coming out of a doorway and I asked if he'd found anything important. "I'm afraid not," he replied with a friendly smile. "And I'm not the secret villain if that's what you're thinking! I was only in Marilla's room to check for splinters."

I was dismayed to realize he'd also been given Matthew's clue and exchanged an unhappy glance with Makiko. There were only hooks on the walls of Marilla's bedroom so we hurried across the hallway to another room, where a big wardrobe stood in one corner.

"Bingo! We did it, Makiko."

Recalling Matthew's instructions that we should "around the walls search out a clue," we began examining the outside of the wardrobe, then Makiko opened the doors. "He also speak of somewhere dark. Is pitcher black inside."

"You mean pitch black," I said, smiling. "Okay, let's check but I hope there aren't spiders inside this thing."

The wardrobe was big enough for both of us but I felt suddenly nervous. What if someone slammed the doors and locked us in? Quickly I ran my hands over the walls, just wanting to get out of there, but Makiko worked more patiently and was rewarded.

"Here is clue, Austen-san!" Kneeling down, she studied a slip of paper stapled to the inner wall of the wardrobe. "Is so dark to read."

I opened both doors wide to get more light into the wardrobe, then knelt down. Squinting my eyes I read the clue aloud:

> "Among you lurks one whose sight
> Is fixed on evil deeds this night;
> But the villain's heart churns with fear
> Because to the truth you now draw near."

I grinned. "We're getting close, Makiko!"

"Is sincerely to be hoped, but what of clue? Means what?"

"To tell the truth, I just don't know." I read the clue once more, then closed the wardrobe doors. In my pocket I found some paper, ripped off a tiny piece and slipped it into the space between the doors. "Let's check this later."

"For what reason?"

"If the paper's still between the doors we'll know they haven't been opened and nobody else has found that particular clue."

We remained in the bedroom for a few minutes, totally stumped about our next move, then decided to return downstairs to see how the others were doing. Several people were sitting in the parlour and dining room looking unhappy as they were served tea by Aaron.

"What's wrong with them?" I whispered.

He smiled. "They're dead."

"Huh?"

"You'll croak, too, if you get a deadly note so be careful. Remember you don't have to read anything if you're suspicious."

I tried to get more details but Aaron moved on with his teapot while Katie passed out pieces of cake. I reached hungrily for some, hoping it wouldn't be poisoned, then accepted a cup and saucer from the girl who was Anne. As I waited for Aaron to return with the teapot I noticed that Makiko had received an upside-down cup. Warning bells rang in my head but, before I could speak, she lifted the cup and saw a note.

"Oh no," she said, reading it. "Death has arrived."

I was really disappointed as she slumped down in a chair. I'd lost my friend and fellow detective and now I was alone, one of the few remaining guests with a chance of unmasking the killer. As I glumly pondered my next move I happened to notice Miss Martin heading for the stairs.

She looked so furtive that I decided to follow. Upstairs I peeked at her inside Marilla's bedroom but she was only looking out at the night, so I went to check the wardrobe and discovered the slip of paper still in place.

Then I glanced across the hallway and realized something was wrong.

Miss Martin had gone to the bureau and was staring at a slip of paper she'd picked up. Her whole body was trembling and her face was white. As I watched, one hand went to her throat.

"What is it, Miss Martin?"

"I . . . please, I need . . ."

Rushing into the room, I helped her to a chair. For a moment I studied her face, wondering if she was having a heart attack, then glanced at the paper in her hand. Printed on it was a single word: REVENGE.

"Miss Martin, what does this mean? Is it part of the game?"

"No." She shook her head. "No, this note isn't anything to do with my Mystery Weekend."

"Then who left it here?"

"I . . ." She took a deep breath. "We must continue with the game. I shall not let anyone spoil the evening."

"But what about this note?"

"Leave me alone," she said sharply. "Go downstairs. Matthew is waiting to continue the game."

There was no arguing so I did as she ordered. Perhaps I should have told Matthew something was wrong but the moment I entered the parlour he nodded to 'Cameron of the Yard,' who began asking those of us still alive about the death notes received by people like Makiko. I think he was hinting there was a pattern to how the notes were delivered, but I was too worried about Miss Martin to concentrate. I looked at Makiko, wondering if I was allowed to speak to her when she was officially dead, then saw the old man hobble my way on his silver-headed cane.

"Please help me, young lady. I'm not feeling well."

I looked at him suspiciously but his green eyes seemed so innocent I realized the game was making me paranoid. "Next I'll be suspecting Matthew," I said, smiling. "How can I help you, sir?"

"Please escort me to my car. I'll rest there for a spell. My wife warned me the excitement would be hard for my heart but I couldn't miss this Mystery Weekend. Isn't it fun?"

As we went outside I looked for the umpire but there was no sign of him. The moment the old man had sunk onto his car's seat, sighing with relief, I hurried back to Green Gables, anxious to return to my detective work. But when I got inside the guests were still downstairs answering the Inspector's questions and he asked me to join them. I listened carefully as he discussed the evidence, knowing he was dropping important hints, and then I jumped with fright.

Someone was pounding on the outside door.

5

Even the Inspector was startled.

He exchanged a puzzled look with Matthew, then went into the hallway to answer the door. He returned with a heavy man in a Mountie's uniform with leather dress gloves. "Good evening," the officer said, removing his police cap to reveal a meagre crop of hair. "Which one of you phoned?"

People looked at each other with puzzled faces then one man smiled. "I suppose you're involved in the game! For a moment I was worried."

"What game?"

"Ah, you're playing innocent. Are you going to question us just like Cameron of the Yard?"

But the Mountie appeared to be genuinely puzzled and I realized he was either the real thing or an excellent actor. “Headquarters just received a call about trouble,” he said, studying us with his blue eyes. “I was patrolling in the area so I was radioed to investigate.”

Moving closer to Aaron I whispered, “Is this part of the Mystery Weekend?”

“I don’t think so.”

The Mountie looked at Cameron of the Yard. “Is anyone else in this house?”

“Only Miss Martin. She’s upstairs, waiting until I’ve finished questioning everyone. Then she’ll . . .”

“I’d better go and get her, too.” The Mountie started for thc stairs, then paused. “Everyone remain here. That’s an order.”

The moment he was gone I studied the others. The faces of most were genuinely blank, but I noticed the young priest whispering urgently to the woman in sandals. I moved closer, hoping to overhear them, but the priest got up and went to the dining-room table to pour himself morc tca. Sitting down on the sofa I smiled at the woman.

“I’m pretty sure you’re the killer, but I’m not saying anything to Miss Martin until I’m absolutely certain.”

Her laugh was phoney. “Me a killer? I’m just a tourist.”

“Where are you from?”

“Um, Nova Scotia. A place called, uh, Lunenburg—you’ve probably never heard of it.”

“Lunenburg! I’ve been there!”

She looked surprised. “Oh, uh, how nice.”

“What do you think of the school? Isn’t it weird?”

“You mean the, um, architecture? Those unusual windows?”

"No, I mean the cemetery beside the school. It's so creepy."

"Oh, I see." Her face was beginning to glow. "I guess I've never noticed the cemetery."

"That's strange, when it's right in the middle of Lunenburg." I leaned back on the sofa, convinced that she'd lied about being a tourist, then noticed no one was speaking. Quickly I tried to find some chatter.

"I love all the old things in this place. What's the story on the typewriter in the hallway?"

"It belonged to Maud."

"Is it valuable?"

She nodded. "A thief could collect a lot of money for that typewriter from a crooked collector."

"I'm surprised it's not under lock and key. Maybe there's a link between this Mystery Weekend and . . ."

But I never completed my sentence. The Mountie appeared suddenly in the doorway with his face showing the effects of a terrible shock.

"Miss Martin is dead."

For a moment there was a stunned silence, then the priest jumped up. "You must be joking! That's not possible."

"Why?" The officer's voice was sharp. "What do you know about this?"

"Nothing." Quickly the priest sat down. "Nothing of course. I'm only an actor—my name's A.P. Cole, you've probably heard of me. I'm just playing a role, nothing more."

The Mountie continued to stare at him, then his eyes went slowly around the room. Some people like the redhead and the man with pale eyes looked at the floor but others returned the Mountie's gaze. I was aware of the loud ticking of the clock and the thumping of my heart. Were we still playing the game, or was Miss Martin really dead?

"I'm going to radio headquarters for more officers." The Mountie put on his uniform cap. "Everyone remain exactly where you are."

When the door closed behind him there was a long silence, then everyone began talking at once. Several people glanced at the ceiling and I knew they wanted to go upstairs to check on Miss Martin, but the Mountie had spoken with such authority that no one dared move. A few minutes later the door opened and we all turned toward the sound, expecting to see more police officers, but it was only the old man. His eyes were bright with excitement.

"Is it true? I spoke to that policeman and he claims Miss Martin is *dead*. But how's that possible?"

"Nobody knows," replied the woman in sandals. "We've been ordered to stay right here—so you'd better take a chair."

I sat down beside Makiko and gave her a worried smile, hoping that somehow Miss Martin was safe, but then I remembered the revenge note. My whole body suddenly went cold, and I knew in my heart that she really was dead.

"It's awful," I moaned. "I just can't believe it."

Everyone was upset so we were a miserable lot when sirens finally sounded in the night and came rapidly closer. I expected the police investigation to be led by the heavy Mountie, but a young woman wearing lavender eyeshadow and pretty lipstick was the first through the door, followed by two officers I didn't recognize. The parlour seemed jammed with people as they listened to Cameron of the Yard and Matthew explain they were actors involved in the Mystery Weekend.

Then the officers asked us for details of what had happened and, as more sirens wailed closer, one went upstairs to investigate. When she returned her face was solemn. "It looks as though Miss Martin died of a drug overdose."

"What?" A.P. Cole appeared horrified. "But that's impossible!"

"Why?"

"Because, well . . ."

Matthew raised his hand. "Because Miss Martin never even used aspirin. What kind of drugs are you talking about?"

"Heroin."

He shook his head. "I can't believe it."

"It may have been suicide, but I suspect murder."

A wave of shock and horror ran though the room. A.P. Cole rose out of his chair, staring at the Mountie, then slumped back with his mouth hanging open. His reaction was the most dramatic, perhaps because he was an actor, but other people were equally shaken.

"*Murder?*" The colour had drained from 'Cameron of the Yard's' beefy face, making it whiter than his moustache. "From the time she went upstairs until her body was discovered not one of us left here."

The old man raised his hand. "I went outside to my car."

"That's true, but nobody went up those stairs. Miss Martin was completely alone."

"Perhaps someone was hiding in a closet," the man with pale eyes suggested, "then attacked her."

"This house doesn't have closets," I pointed out, "and the only wardrobe was empty. I can guarantee that."

"What about the attic?" Katie asked.

"We'll check it," the Mountie replied, "but no one would hide up there after committing murder because it's such an obvious place for us to look."

"Could the murderer have climbed out of a window?"

Aaron shook his head. "The windows and back door are specially sealed with burglar alarms—there are lots of valuable things in Green Gables. Miss Martin explained the security to me while we were preparing the house for this evening's events."

The Mounties exchanged glances, obviously puzzled. "Everything points to murder, but the killer would have had to come down those stairs in front of you all. And no one noticed anything."

Matthew nodded. "Like I said, we were all here together. Nobody could have left without the rest of us knowing."

I looked at the officer. "I just remembered something." Quickly I told her about the revenge note and Miss Martin's reaction. The Mountie said she'd seen the note upstairs and agreed it could be important, but the others didn't seem interested. A.P. Cole even had the nerve to scoff at my theory.

"The note was probably part of the game," he said. "I told Miss Martin she shouldn't let you kids sign up for the Mystery Weekend. It's my opinion that . . ."

But the Mountie cut him off by turning to Matthew. "You say an officer discovered the body?"

"Yes."

"Okay, I'll check with headquarters." She looked around. "You'll have to stay until we take statements, then you can go home. Naturally you must remain on the island until further notice."

It was some time before I was able to leave the house with Makiko. Her father was waiting outside and so were all kinds of media types. Green Gables was lit up by bright TV lights as reporters moved in. When one of them came up to me I did what the Mountie had requested and replied, "No comment." Then I hurried to the car with Makiko and her father. As he pulled away from Green Gables I felt horrible thinking about Miss Martin.

Nobody had expected to be dealing with a *real* murder tonight.

* * *

Throughout the night I kept trying to solve the puzzle of how someone could have reached Miss Martin in that upstairs room. Surely there was a solution but I couldn't find it. When dawn came I was awake, so for once I didn't mind the roosters crowing, Rusty the dog barking, and the hogs making disgusting throaty noises like a bunch of elephants gargling.

My digital clock read 6:33 as the tractor roared into life. I struggled sleepily into my jeans and T-shirt and went outside to help bring the cows in from a nearby field. I probably wasn't much help, but I smiled encouragingly at my host, Alvin, and his sons while the cows wandered slowly home, their breath steaming in the chilly morning air. Then, as a million birds twittered from the power lines and the PEI flag fluttered above the yard, the boys brought the morning's first warm milk from the barn for the cats to enjoy.

Finally it was our turn to eat and we went into the kitchen where Alvin's wife, Eleanor, had thick sausages frying on the stove. When everyone was sitting down I broke the news about Miss Martin's death. Alvin immediately picked up the local newspaper and read us an anonymous "Letter to the Editor" that was super critical of Miss Martin's plans for her Mystery Weekend, calling her a snollygoster for managing to get permission to use Green Gables.

"I've heard that weird word somewhere before," I said to Eleanor. "What's it mean?"

"A person who's shrewd and calculating, and doesn't care about the common good."

"What a terrible thing to call Miss Martin."

She nodded her head. "There was a lot of controversy about her plans for Green Gables, but I can't believe that's why she was murdered."

"This creep didn't even have the courage to sign the letter," I said, smacking the newspaper with my hand. I was preparing to let fly with a few strong opinions when a knock on the door announced Makiko's arrival for a visit. There was some good-natured joking about her being 'from away,' and Alvin claimed that even I had an accent, then he smiled at Makiko.

"I imagine you'd like to visit the place where Maud actually wrote *Anne of Green Gables*."

"All guidebooks say farmhouse gone."

"There's still the foundations to see if you'd like to."

"Oh yes!" Makiko's eyes were shining. "Yes please."

Outside the house dark clouds were gathering over the sea. "It'll be a poor day to set a hen," Alvin said as he started the pickup, then looked unhappily in his mirror at the blue exhaust smoke. "This thing burns too much oil." While we drove the short distance into Cavendish he talked proudly about his beautiful island's fifty-six shades of green and then pointed at a small house that was the local post office.

"If you mail your postcards from there they'll be stamped Green Gables PEI. It's an exact replica of the place where Maud lived while writing her book about Anne. Her grandparents ran the post office in their home and she helped out."

"Is second most thrilling post office for me to visit," Makiko said. "First thrilling is at top of Mount Fuji after I climb hours with friends."

"You can mail letters from up on that volcano?"

She laughed. "Oh yes. Plus visit shrines and souvenir shops."

"Amazing."

Soon we'd climbed over a rusty barbed-wire fence and were struggling through thick woods with heavy undergrowth. Alvin pointed out the shrivelled remains of apple trees that had surrounded the farmhouse and then we reached the site. I was kind of disappointed because there was only a bunch of big mossy stones where Maud's house had once stood so I was ready to leave after I'd taken a picture. But then I saw Makiko standing still with her eyes squeezed shut and her hands clasped tightly to her tummy.

"What's wrong?"

"Austen-san, is moment of joy." Handing me her camera, she climbed onto the foundation. "Please to photograph me with memories of famous Maud. In this exact spot red-haired Anne born." As the camera clicked she looked at a bird chirping merrily in a tree. "Now this place forever mine."

Alvin smiled at her. "You Japanese folks sure love that story. Maud's success is kind of nice."

"It's neat when people's dreams come true." I thought about Miss Martin, finding it hard to believe she'd been with us only yesterday. "The Mystery Weekend was a great dream. I just *know* I can figure out who was responsible for this tragedy."

"Perhaps that's so Liz, but be careful. This isn't a game you're playing any more. If you get involved, it could mean big trouble for you."

6

It started to rain just after we got back to Parkview Farm, so Makiko and I stayed indoors talking about our schools and families, and becoming closer friends. I discovered she was also studying French and Russian, and Makiko laughed at the plastic lobster I'd been sent by my brother Tom. In its belly was a magnifying glass "to help your search for clues in PEI."

"Speaking of detective work, you know what bothers me? We never learned the solution to the Mystery Weekend."

"Villain was sandals-woman I am believing."

"You're probably right. She's a really suspicious type."

Late in the afternoon the rain clouds rolled away. Rusty came outside with us and sat on my foot as I rubbed him under the chin. The cows were grazing in a field of amazing green; beyond them the sea was lashed with whitecaps. Surf crashed and thundered against the coast as we stood there silently, just staring.

"Such beauty," Makiko said at last. "Is island of dreams."

Makiko's father arrived shortly after to take us for dinner. During the drive Mr. Tanaka told me about the 'plum rains' which come at the beginning of summer in Japan, then explained why he was in PEI. "I come each year to buy tuna at North Lake. It is shipped to Japan for sushi."

"What's that?"

"A favourite food. Tiny portions of raw fish on a bed of rice."

"Raw fish? Are you kidding?"

He smiled. "You must visit Kyoto one day. I will prepare sushi for you myself."

Makiko nodded. "Oh please Austen-san! We climb Mount Fuji together."

"Hold it! You're asking me to eat raw fish and climb a volcano? What kind of holiday is that?"

They both laughed. "If you wish," Mr. Tanaka said, "we can take you instead to *Makudonarudo*."

"What's that?"

"McDonald's."

"You've got the golden arches over there? Okay, maybe I will visit!"

We stopped the car along the way to take pictures of red roads wandering across vast fields and fishing boats at anchor in peaceful coves. Then we finally arrived at Shaw's Hotel, where Makiko and her father were staying. It was the island's oldest hotel, built in

1860, with one big residence and several cottages and a barn, all surrounded by grass that sloped gently to an arm of the sea. The dining room extended out from one wall like a ship's bow and was enclosed by picture windows overlooking the lawn and shimmering water. Big bouquets of flowers stood around the walls and there were smaller arrangements on each table.

"Strawberry soup tonight," the waitress said to Makiko. "Your favourite."

"Good news!" She grinned at me. "But perhaps not for Austen-san? Raw strawberries, I must warn."

"Hey, I can take it. I've even been known to try raw cow juice."

"Please?"

"You know, milk." As we grinned at each other I helped myself to a chunk of homemade bread from a basket on the table, then spread it with the yellowest butter I'd ever seen. "Fabulous! This stuff even *tastes* yellow." I licked my lips when the soup arrived. "Eleanor keeps telling me not to stog myself but the sea air gives me an enormous appetite. Anyway, that's my excuse and I'm sticking to it!"

"Stog yourself?" Mr. Tanaka asked.

"It means overeating." Quickly I polished off the pink soup, which tasted deliciously of strawberries. "I've learned some unusual expressions lately, like snollygoster. That means a shrewd type, but I doubt if many people even know the word."

Outside the window some kids were doing cartwheels, and a tortoise-shell cat strolled past lazily. I nudged Makiko. "Isn't she a beauty?"

"Oh yes. Japanese believe such cat bring good fortune."

"Probably because tortoise-shells are born only female. How can they lose, right?"

"Also maybe . . ."

She paused to look across the crowded dining room at the familiar face of the redhead who'd been at the Mystery Weekend. Tonight she looked spectacular in diamonds and an emerald dress. Practically every man in the room, including Mr. Tanaka, stared as she and her companion were escorted toward a table. Then she noticed us and came over to say hello, introducing herself as Breanne Short.

"This is my husband, Francis," she added. "He's a seventh-generation Islander, as I proudly tell everyone."

I glanced at Mr. Short's hand and noticed there wasn't a wedding ring, then studied his face. His brown eyes were large and seemed friendly, but small veins showed on the surface of his cheeks and I suspected that his perfect white teeth were "store bought," as Eleanor would say. He seemed too old for Breanne but, as she stood there raving about their happy marriage, I decided it was none of my business. Then she looked at me with a smile.

"You're staring at my eyes, Liz. Do they surprise you?"

"Sort of, I guess. Not many people have one blue eye and one green."

"Actually, both of them are green. I used to wear glasses but now I have contact lenses."

"Me too, but they don't change the colour of my eyes."

"My regular contacts are clear plastic, but I also have a blue set. I'm a professional singer and sometimes I wear them onstage, or when I'm working as a model. This evening one of my clear lenses popped out and I couldn't find it so I'm wearing a blue lens until we get home."

"Why didn't you wear both blue contacts?"

She winked at her husband. "We've been married so long I believe Francis needs something to think about over dinner. It'll be fun to decide which eye he gazes into the most."

He laughed. "Breanne had good news today. She's been signed for the role of Marilla in the Festival musical. As you likely know, Miss Martin played that part for years."

"But," Makiko said, "you have much too pretty face for Marilla."

"How sweet of you. Actually it's amazing what professional make-up can do. A wig and powder and black eyeliner will make me old, just wait and see. Have you got tickets?"

Mr. Tanaka shook his head. "Unhappily I waited too long. Now all seats are sold."

"Perhaps I can arrange something."

"Most kind of you."

"Marilla is a good part," I said. "You must be excited."

"I admit that I'm pleased."

"Have you come to Shaw's Hotel for a fancy dinner to celebrate?"

She blushed. "Very clever. I didn't think it was appropriate because of Miss Martin's death but Francis insisted."

I watched them walk away, then glanced at Makiko. "I guess every cloud has a silver lining."

"Please?"

"It's nothing, Makiko. Just an expression."

* * *

Driving back to Cavendish I studied the dark shoreline and the squiggly clouds scattered across the red sky. We parked in the church lot, already crowded with cars as people arrived for the memorial service, then walked to the cemetery to put flowers on Maud's grave. I watched Mr. Tanaka arrange them with great ceremony, then looked down the slope to the woods.

"Makiko! It's that umpire again."

He'd appeared from among the trees with something in his hand. It was too dark to see what he was carrying as he moved quickly past the abandoned shack toward a distant corner of the graveyard. I wanted to stay but Mr. Tanaka was anxious about being late for the service, so I took a last reluctant look at the umpire as we headed for the church.

It was packed, and we were lucky to discover a place near the front. I noticed with interest that my softball coach had come with Humphrey, then studied a stained-glass window dedicated to the memory of Maud, and an antique organ near it.

"Do you think she played that?" I whispered to Makiko.

"Is probable. Picture of her next to organ."

"You're right." Maud smiled shyly from under a big hat in the portrait, a bouquet of roses in her hands.

"What a thrill to visit her own church!"

Some important-looking people from the government were ushered in, then the choir appeared wearing black robes with green at the neck. I noticed Aaron and Eleanor immediately, then someone I didn't expect: the woman in sandals. She'd actually worn them to this service!

The minister was really nice, explaining that we had gathered to praise the beauty God gave the world in the person of Maud and her writings. "We are all kindred spirits here tonight," he said, "drawn together by her love of nature and her acute understanding of people." A young woman read a psalm with great feeling and we heard Maud's Island Hymn. After some local kids received special creative writing awards something neat happened: flowers were presented to the church by a grey-haired woman who'd actually met the author as a child. "She always called herself Maud. My mother went to school with her, and I remember hearing how Maud entertained her classmates with stories while they sat by the brook at lunchtime. It was the greatest moment of my life when I met this famous woman."

I stared at her in awe and hoped I'd have a chance after the service to ask more about her brush with history, but by the time I reached the church basement she was already surrounded by people asking questions and I couldn't get near. Instead I inspected a long table spread with goodies, including a cake in the shape of Green Gables, then waited impatiently until Aaron arrived. We talked for a while, then watched happily as Makiko was asked to officially cut the

Green Gables cake because she'd come to the memorial service from so far away. Among the first to receive a piece of cake was the woman in sandals, so I decided to ask Aaron for an introduction.

Her name was Sabrina, which she immediately told me means 'a princess.' She didn't seem like royalty to me, with her dirty toenails and hair that needed washing, but of course I didn't say so. I pressed her for details about the Mystery Weekend and was delighted when she admitted lying about being a tourist.

"I've never been to Lunenburg so you did catch me with that business about the cemetery. You're not a bad detective Lisa, but . . ."

"It's Liz."

"What?"

"My name's Liz, not Lisa."

"Whatever." Yawning, she looked across the room at Aaron, who was helping Makiko pass out cake. Waving him over, she grabbed a second big piece and took a hefty bite. "If you're such a great detective guess my age. I'll bet twenty dollars you can't."

"No problem." I studied her face, noticing especially the bags under her bloodshot eyes. "Let's see, I think . . ."

"Time's up. You lose."

"What?"

"You owe me twenty bucks. Let's have it."

"You've got to be kidding."

"No money, eh? Kids these days are so cheap, but I won't forget you owe me." Sabrina downed a glass of punch in a single swallow, then wiped her mouth with the back of her hand. "Obviously it was only a lucky guess when you said I was the Mystery Weekend villain."

"So you really were?"

"Oh yes. I stabbed the captain and then . . ."

"Makiko figured that out. I can't wait to tell her!"

"You know," she said with a forced smile. "I really wish you'd stop interrupting all the time."

"Sorry."

"At Green Gables I had most of the guests polished off with my deadly notes. If that Mountie hadn't arrived to spoil the game you'd have died next."

"Maybe yes, maybe no." Sabrina was rapidly making my blood boil. "We'd already found the note in the wardrobe that said we were close to solving the case."

"I bet you were stumped by that clue."

"At the time, yes. But I thought about it last night in bed. When it said 'the villain's heart churns with fear,' did that refer to the butter churn in the kitchen?"

Her eyes actually bulged. "How'd you know that?"

Grinning, I tapped my head. "Those little grey cells, you know. I bet if I'd looked in that churn I'd have solved the Mystery Weekend."

I was anxious to share the news with Makiko but she was in the opposite corner, talking to the province's Lieutenant-Governor. Meanwhile, Sabrina looked so disgruntled that I felt a bit guilty. "You're a good actor, actually. Are you in the cast of the musical?"

"Nope, and I've never acted before. When I first moved to PEI I lived in Cavendish, so I've stayed in the choir here, but a few months ago I got a job at a store in Charlottetown. When I started rooming with

Miss Martin she asked me to do the Mystery Weekend."

"Will you move now?"

Sabrina shook her head. "I'll have the place all to myself. It'll be lovely, especially after the cat's gone."

"What do you mean?"

"I hate cats. Tomorrow I'll advertise Miss Martin's Siamese, and sell it to the first person who comes to the door."

I was so shocked that I was speechless. I got away from Sabrina as quickly as possible but I must have looked terrible because my coach called me over. "Liz, what's wrong?"

I told her about the Siamese and begged for permission to take it home to Winnipeg, but she looked doubtful. "What would your parents say?"

"They wouldn't mind at all, Sandra. They adore cats."

"Well maybe, but I'll have to phone them for permission." She then introduced me to the person beside her, the pale-eyed man with the beard who'd arrived late at the Mystery Weekend. "Mr. Isaac used to work with my Mom in Winnipeg. Small world, eh?"

I nodded. "Sorry I didn't say much at the softball diamond, sir. I'm not supposed to speak to strangers."

"Don't apologize. You did the right thing."

"Do you live on the island?"

"No, I'm here on business. I'm a television producer and would like to do a show about Maud's life. I'm scouting the island for locations and background material." He sipped some punch. "I was just telling Sandra that tomorrow I'm going to Confederation Centre in Charlottetown to examine their collection of Maud's papers."

Sandra smiled. "Mr. Isaac's got special permission to see the actual manuscript of *Anne of Green Gables.* He invited me along but I've got a date with Humphrey."

"How about you, young lady? Care to see some literary history?"

"You bet!" I smiled. "My friend Makiko would go crazy to see that manuscript. Could she come, too?"

"Of course."

We made arrangements, then Mr. Isaac went off to talk to the grey-haired lady who'd met Maud. Just then I noticed a faint blush spread across Sandra's face, and I turned around to see Humphrey walking toward us. Pleased to see Cupid succeeding, I gave him a big smile.

"It's good to see you again."

"Ditto, Liz." His green eyes seemed a bit bleary as he squinted at me through his thick glasses. "I've s-s-some good news," he stammered. "You and S-S-Sandra can watch the musical from backstage."

"Wonderful! I can't wait."

Humphrey handed Sandra a plate of sandwiches. "I s-s-selected the nicest ones."

"Aren't you eating anything?"

Smiling, Humphrey ran a hand over his big tummy. "I sh-sh-should try jogging like you. Then I could eat without it sh-sh-showing." He sipped some fruit punch, then turned to me. "You were at Green Gables last night? A terrible tragedy. I knew Miss Martin, of course, from working backstage at the Festival. We'll all miss her s-s-so much."

"I wonder how Miss Martin would have felt if I'd solved the butter churn clue? She was a bit crabby but I think she'd have been pleased."

"You got that one? Good for you—it was difficult."

Hoping to impress him further, I talked about some real detective work I'd done at places like Lunenburg. Humphrey listened with interest, but then he suggested I'd only succeeded because of my brother's help.

"I can s-s-see my opinion annoys you Liz, but I'm an old-fashioned man. You women sh-sh-should leave police work alone. That Mountie will have trouble s-s-solving Miss Martin's murder, and wearing lavender eyeshadow won't help her at all I'm afraid."

I knew he was joking but his comments were like a red flag to a bull. I charged at him with a million facts about female brainpower and only shut up when Makiko arrived carrying a large piece of cake.

"Please to try, Austen-san. Is indeed toothsome."

I laughed. "What a great word." After introducing my coach and Humphrey, I told them about the sushi I'd been invited to sample in Kyoto. Humphrey said he'd tried sushi and liked it, then talked about the island's famous lobster suppers.

"Have you attended one, Makiko?"

"I regret not."

"I think a treat is in order." He smiled at the three of us. "Perhaps you'd all join me for a s-s-supper tomorrow evening? I know a church group that s-s-serves delicious lobster, and it would be a way to apologize to Liz for my unkind remarks."

"Thanks Humphrey," I said, "that's a really super idea."

It *was* a nice thought, but I was still simmering when I arrived back at Parkview Farm. Before going inside I sat on a lawn chair and rubbed Rusty's head while I looked at the stars, so bright in the night sky. Then, as the wind rustled nearby bushes and warm air brushed against my face, I made a silent vow: somehow I'd solve the riddle of Miss Martin's death and show Humphrey he'd been wrong.

7

"You know something about PEI? Even the ditches are beautiful."

I said this as we drove toward Charlottetown in Mr. Isaac's luxurious car. Purple and white and pink flowers blossomed on tall plants at the roadside, dancing in the wash of air from passing traffic. "I wonder if that's Lady's Slipper? We learned in school it's the provincial flower."

Mr. Isaac shook his head. "You're looking at wild lupines. Did you know that every spring the people here have a clean-up day? They pick the litter out of every ditch on the island, which is why it's all so spotless."

Makiko smiled. "Island paradise. Every day in diary I try new words for saying my love of Anne island but famous Maud say everything best."

"Seeing her manuscript should be a treat," Mr. Isaac said. "I've often wondered if she wrote that story straight off or made a lot of changes." He was silent for a while, then smiled as we passed yet another field of low plants with pale blue blossoms. "What would the island do without its potatoes, right?"

"And tourists," I said. "Have you seen the musical yet?"

He nodded. "Strangely enough I saw the last production before Miss Martin's death. She was still a dandy actress."

"You'd seen her act before?"

There was a long silence and I had the feeling he didn't want to answer my question. But I kept looking at him and eventually he said, "Oh yes, back in Ontario."

"In a musical?"

He shrugged. "It was so long ago I can't remember."

"She was young then, I guess. Was she attractive?"

Again he was silent before finally answering, "She was quite nice, actually. I was sorry to find she'd aged so, but I suppose the years are hard on most people."

I turned to Makiko. "I remember in the woods Miss Martin said life can be difficult." Glancing at Mr. Isaac I added, "Especially where men are concerned."

He looked annoyed. "Typical! Molly always blamed her problems on others but she caused most of them herself. I shouldn't speak ill of the dead but once she turned in a fellow actor to the police. He'd fought someone outside a pub and the man died. Molly was the only witness, but she didn't say a word until a reward was offered. The actor was an expert on make-up and disguises so he'd gone into hiding using a new identity. When Molly heard about the money she tipped off the police about his disguise and they found him."

"Was he sent to prison?"

Mr. Isaac nodded. "For a long time, but I guess he'd be out by now."

"Excuse me for saying this but you sound kind of angry. Do you think the man shouldn't have gone to prison?"

"Of course not, but even after all these years it still upsets me to think of Molly's part in the whole thing."

"You mean how she stayed silent until there was a reward?"

"Yes," he said, then added, "let's just drop the subject."

I was dying to know if Makiko was wondering how he knew so much about Miss Martin's past, too, but of course I couldn't say anything. Shortly after we passed the University of PEI and entered the city. I smiled at Makiko as we passed *Makudonarudo*, then we hung a right and were soon in a residential area that was like a dream world. Massive trees shaded ancient houses with verandahs and stone chimneys and towers with mysterious windows. Kids and dogs played in leafy parks, then I saw a church spire that soared towards the rain clouds high above.

"That's the Kirk of Saint James," Mr. Isaac said. "It has a ghost story that I'd love to use in my TV production but I can't find proof Maud ever attended services there."

"What's the story?"

"Back in 1853 a terrible storm battered the area. Someone saw three barefooted women enter the kirk, and then its bell began tolling. When the minister investigated no one was inside, but later he learned a steamer called the Fairy Queen had sunk exactly when the bell began tolling."

"Who were the women?"

"Nobody knows, but after the storm three women in the church congregation learned they'd become widows."

"Spooky." I stared at the walls of red stone until the kirk was out of sight, then shook my head. "I'd never go in there."

"Sandra says you're extremely courageous."

"Maybe, but ghosts freak me."

"Okay then, how about visiting a school?"

"But it's summer holidays. That freaks me even more!"

Mr. Isaac laughed. "Later today I'll be looking at L.M. Montgomery School. On her birthday the students and teachers wear old-fashioned clothes and eat homemade ice cream. A slate is baked out of biscuit dough and painted black, then one of the kids gets to break it over the principal's head."

"It sounds great!"

We entered the downtown area, where only a single hotel could be called a high-rise. Most of the other buildings were out of the past with curved windows in their brick walls, and some even had stone faces carved into their walls. Mr. Isaac pointed out a pharmacy that had been operating so long its customers included the first Canadian prime minister, then he pulled to a stop.

"That's Confederation Centre," he said, motioning toward a group of modern buildings. "It was designed to celebrate the one hundredth birthday of the meeting which led to the creation of Canada."

"Is that where we'll see the musical?"

He nodded. "Besides the theatre there's an art gallery and a library and the place where Maud's papers are stored."

All kinds of people were hanging around the Centre's open plaza enjoying some free entertainment, including a guy who was using two sticks to keep a third one spinning in the air. Above his head Norse ships and setting suns and prairie lilies danced on provincial flags that cracked in the wind. Then, all of a sudden, it started to rain and everyone went racing for cover, except two girls who raised their arms in an exuberant dance as the huge drops lashed down.

Inside the Centre I shook the rain out of my hair, then we followed a friendly woman down a labyrinth of stairwells and tunnels under the Centre until we arrived in a large storage room. I'd expected the manuscript to be in a heavily-guarded vault but it was just in a box on a shelf. "How exciting," Mr. Isaac murmured, as he lifted the lid and we saw the slightly discoloured page with the opening chapter title in Maud's spidery handwriting: *Mrs. Rachel Lynde is Surprised.*

"She did edit her work, Mr. Isaac. Look how she wrote 'the Avonlea road' in the first sentence, then made it into the main road. Plus there's more."

We examined some of Maud's scrapbooks, which were full of flowers she'd preserved and a lot of cat pictures. "She'd never have sold a Siamese," I said to Makiko as we turned the pages, reading her early poetry and newspaper articles about "local teacher Miss

Lucy M. Montgomery" fast becoming popular with her scholars.

Mr. Isaac settled down to make notes, so we arranged to meet later and were taken by our escort through more tunnels and up a flight of stairs to a door opening onto a side street. The rain had stopped and we stepped into a freshly-washed, sunny world. As we were discussing our plans I saw two familiar people approaching. One was Breanne, the red-headed singer, and beside her was my coach's sister, Katie.

"We're going to a rehearsal of the musical," Katie said, then added, "Have you heard about A.P. Cole? He's so upset about Miss Martin's death that he called in sick. He won't be doing the musical all this week."

"That's strange," I said, recalling the actor's attitude toward Miss Martin in the woods. "I can't believe they were exactly buddies."

"You're right. People were surprised when she asked him to be in her Mystery Weekend. They were often at each other's throats, but he *is* a talented actor. I guess she really needed him."

"Do you know where A.P. Cole lives?"

"In Ma Gertrude's Rooming House on Sydney Street." She pointed at the crosses on distant twin spires. "Over near that basilica."

I looked at Makiko. "Let's go say hi. Maybe he needs someone to buy him chicken soup and aspirin."

Katie looked concerned. "Are you sure that's a good idea? I mean, maybe you shouldn't bother him."

I smiled. "Oh, we won't bother him. Besides, we have some detective work to do, and that's right on our way."

* * *

Minutes later we were standing outside of the rooming house. Chunks of paint had peeled off the faded wooden walls, flowers lay dead in a windowsill pot and pieces of a rusty motorcycle were scattered over a lawn that hadn't been cut since the last ice age. "Couldn't A.P. Cole find somewhere better to stay?"

"Actor poor pay. Better to make video camera in nice factory."

"Yeah, but he doesn't seem the type. A face like his deserves to be drooled over on a million screens."

"With respect Austen-san, I find this man have eyes of snake. Cold and watchful."

"Let's just agree we disagree." I looked at the dirty and torn curtains on an upstairs window, wondering if A.P. Cole was watching us. "Let's go offer our condolences on his mysterious illness."

"My skin have tingles."

"Me too, but I'm sure we'll be safe. Ma Gertude is probably a really sweet person who just hasn't found time to clean the curtains lately. Like in the last fifteen years!"

The front hallway smelled of cabbage and old coffee. I looked at the numbers on several doors, then glanced at last year's calendar hanging above a table scattered with mail. A letter from New York City gave me A.P. Cole's room number, plus a thrill when I saw the return address. "Hey Makiko, it's from my favourite soap opera. Why are they writing him?"

"Perhaps offer of job?"

"He'd be great with those eyes. Should we take him this letter?"

"Is private property, Austen-san. If actor not home what then?"

"You're right. We'd better leave it here."

To get to his room we had to climb the stairs to a dim landing, then turn and continue higher. The smell didn't improve and neither did the lighting, so I had to squint at the numbers as we searched for A.P. Cole's room. I knocked timidly at first, then louder when there was no reply. Finally a door opened across thc hallway and a man peered out. He hadn't shaved for several days and he smelled like he hadn't washed for a month.

"What's with all the noise?"

"A.P. Cole is sick and we've come to run his errands."

"Sick? I doubt it. That young man is as healthy as an ox. Now you beat it or I'll call the cops."

His door slammed, making dust swirl around our heads. As we descended the stairs in gloomy silence I heard the outside door click open, followed by footsteps in the lower hallway. Praying the dust wouldn't make us sneeze I gazed down at the woman approaching the table with the mail.

It was Jeni, the bleached-blond we'd seen in the woods with A.P. Cole. Today she wore designer jeans with a fancy T-shirt that read *Beverly Hills*. Wondering where she got her money, I watched her sort through every letter on the table before leaving with one in her pocket.

"I have theory," Makiko whispered, the moment the door closed behind her. "She take soap-opera letter of actor."

"But why? And if she did, where's she going with it?"

"Perhaps we follow?"

"You betcha!"

Stepping outside into blinding sunlight, it took a second before I spotted Jeni walking rapidly south on Sydney Street. "Hurry," I said, afraid that we'd lose her. But I needn't have worried because a wedding party had emerged onto the enormous steps of the basilica and Jeni stopped to watch.

The bride's wedding dress had a long train and the groom was splendid. For a moment I thought he was A.P. Cole, then realized that wasn't likely. Nudging Makiko closer so I could study the bridesmaids' bouquets and bright yellow dresses, I smiled as the happy couple stepped into an old-fashioned buggy pulled by horses with glossy black manes.

"What romance," I sighed. "That's how I want to get married."

"Austen-san, where is quarry?"

I rapidly scanned the people who'd paused to watch the wedding party and then looked up the street with its tall trees and Victorian street lamps. "There she goes!"

Breaking into a run we raced for the spot where I'd glimpsed Jeni disappearing around a corner and almost slammed into her as she gazed into a shop window. We just managed to avoid a collision and tried our best to look innocent as we ran on a short distance before stopping outside a jeweller's window with a glittering display.

"Oh look Makiko, aren't those *glorious* earrings? Wouldn't they look nice on my wedding day?" Moving to another part of the window that was angled in

Jeni's direction I watched her reflection. "That's weird," I whispered. "She's spending forever looking at a display of books but she sure doesn't seem the type. I bet she gave up reading when she couldn't figure out why the cow jumped over the moon."

"Let us continue walking, Austen-san."

"Good strategy. We'll keep an eye on her reflection in the windows."

Just as we passed the side door of the Confederation Centre, Mr. Isaac came out. Makiko and I exchanged a glance, and I knew we were both wondering if we should tell him about A.P. Cole's letter, but we kept quiet as Mr. Isaac talked excitedly about some things in Maud's scrapbooks. Then he left us to visit the basilica.

"Makiko," I whispered as he walked up the street, "he's heading in Jeni's direction. What if they talk about us?"

I couldn't see Mr. Isaac's face as he passed the bookstore but he didn't pause and Jeni continued to stare in the window. Still watching her reflection we moved south to Queen Street where a juggler was entertaining people at an outdoor mall. "There's Matthew and 'Cameron of the Yard,' " I said. "Let's go say hi."

"What of quarry?"

"You're right, we'd better stick with Jeni. But I'd love a chance to talk to those guys. The person who murdered Miss Martin had to be someone at Green Gables, either a guest or an actor, and I'd like to get more information. I just don't understand why someone would want her dead."

"Perhaps for revenge, like the note said?"

"Maybe, or else to profit in some way. I just wish . . ."

But I didn't have a chance to say anything more. Jeni was coming our way in a hurry and I turned to the window display, realizing too late that it showed nothing but hammers and saws and tubs of nails. Hoping she'd think we were into carpentry in a big way I discussed home construction in a loud voice as she passed by, then watched her exchange a few words with a woman pushing a baby carriage.

Just then, a swarm of people got out of a red double-decker bus, so we had lots of cover as Jeni continued west. She passed the tall brick tower of City Hall, then cut left into a residential street. There wasn't much cover so we hung back and pretended to study the houses. Then Makiko touched my arm.

"She approach kirk."

Ahead was the tall spire of the church that Mr. Isaac had been telling us about. Jeni walked to the big wooden door and I shivered as it closed behind her.

"Is she crazy? That place is haunted."

"*Ganbatte,*" Makiko murmured.

"What's that mean?"

"'Press on.' As I climb Mount Fuji I grow weary but friends cry *Ganbatte!* We must not give up, Austen-san."

"No chance of that! What's a ghost or two when we've got each other, right?"

"You betcha."

I laughed out loud, then grinned at Makiko as we approached the kirk. The air inside was chilly and smelled of wood and polish. I squinted, making out the dark oak of the pews and the arches soaring high above. Faint light filtered through the stained-glass windows to show the enormous pipes of an organ, and flags hanging above the pulpit.

I nudged Makiko, nodding in the direction of a woman with a bowed head kneeling in the front pew. The kirk was so large we could have crept closer without being noticed but it wasn't worth the risk. We slipped into the closest pew to watch and wait. After a few minutes my eyes wandered to the rich blues and reds of windows showing a woman with her hand raised in a blessing and another with men crossing the sea.

"Austen-san!"

My eyes snapped to the front pew. Through the dim light I saw the woman preparing to stand up and quickly covered my face, pretending to pray. As footsteps came toward us I slowly parted my fingers and peeked at the woman as she passed. She wore glasses, and her lined face was framed by grey hair.

We'd lost our quarry!

Stunned, I turned to watch the woman leave the kirk and then stared at Makiko. "What happened to Jeni?"

"Sneak out side door?"

"I bet you're right. Come on, maybe we can still catch her."

But there was no sign of a side door, and for a moment we hesitated before deciding to separate in search of an exit. "There's got to be one, Makiko. Give me a shout if you find it."

I watched her pass a colourful arrangement of flowers and disappear into the darkness. Suddenly I felt terribly alone and yet not alone, as if hidden eyes were watching. I swallowed, and tried not to think of the ghosts of those three widows lurking in the darkness. I rubbed my bare arms, wishing the church were warmer, and then tiptoed past a baptismal font toward a golden cross I could see glinting in a dark corner. I was sure I'd either find an exit near the cross or . . .

Just that moment a hand came out of the darkness to grab me!

I screamed so loudly that the shriek echoed and re-echoed from the ceiling and arches. The person stepped closer and I saw Jeni's angry face. "What's going on?" she demanded, squeezing my arm. "I watched in store windows while you two followed me. What's the story?"

"I, uh . . ."

Makiko came out of nowhere to stare at Jeni. "Please," she said, "in my country is wrong to take mail of other person." She pointed at the envelope peeking out of Jeni's hip pocket. "Is not letter of A.P. Cole?"

Jeni just glanced at the letter and muttered something about her boyfriend's mail.

"Don't follow me again," she warned, "or you'll regret it! Do you hear that? Cross me once more and you'll be sorry."

8

It took a long time to recover from the scare we'd been given. Even the milkshakes we drank while discussing Jeni's strange behaviour didn't help much, and we were still confused and shaken when Katie collected us that evening for the drive to the lobster supper at Saint Ann's Church.

My coach was with her sister but she was silent during most of the trip, obviously disappointed because Humphrey hadn't been able to come with us. I was just thinking what a shame it would be if Sandra's heart got broken, when I saw a white horse out my window. As I counted quickly to seven and spit over my baby finger Makiko looked at me with puzzled eyes.

"Please?"

"I do that whenever I see a white horse."

"How know such superstition work?"

"I'm still here aren't I? And that's really saying something after what happened in the kirk." Leaning close I whispered, "Maybe it'll also help Sandra."

She smiled, and I think we both began feeling better. I pointed out the little wooden booths at the end of farm roads, explaining to Makiko that kids waited in them for the school bus during winter storms, then Katie told us about Canada's first car being operated on the island. "But people here didn't like the automobile. Some places wouldn't even allow them to operate, so the owners had to be towed by a horse until they reached a road where driving was allowed."

Sandra chipped in with some stories about a terrible car she'd owned and everyone was laughing by the time we glimpsed Saint Ann's standing alone on a distant slope. "Why lobster?" Sandra asked. "My church doesn't serve meals."

"The ladies started this years ago to pay off the church mortgage, but it was so successful they kept doing it as a fund-raiser."

Next door to the modern church was an attractive house where the priest lived, and a huge parking lot filled with cars and tour buses from many provinces and states. I thought we'd have a long wait for a table but the basement was enormous. A man at an organ played cheerful songs as heaping plates were rushed from the kitchen to the people already seated. There must have been at least a hundred tables, stretching in every direction.

"It's a licence to print money," I exclaimed. "Hey coach, maybe they'll sponsor our team! Let's call ourselves the Manitoba Lobsters, *so tough you can't crack us.*"

Sandra laughed. "As my Mom would say, I'll take it under advisement. Which is a fancy way of saying No Dice."

The moment we'd been seated at a corner table a girl approached with a big smile. "Hi, I'm Sherry, your waitress, and . . ."

"I'm Liz, your customer, and these are my friends."

Sherry gave me a strange look. ". . . and I'd like to welcome you to Saint Ann's lobster supper. I'll be right back to take your order."

As she walked away I whispered, "She thinks we're weird."

"*We're* weird?" Sandra said. "You're the only one who's spoken so far."

"Just having fun." I scanned the crowd of young couples, families with kids, oldsters and long tables of tour groups. "They let in *anyone*," I whispered. "Look at that guy near the organ."

A tubby man with a scruffy beard sat with his back to us knocking back lobster and coffee so fast I wondered if he'd just ended a thirty-day fast. There was a rip in his T-shirt and his jeans were dirty. "Hey Makiko! Maybe that guy's the real Ma Gertrude," I said jokingly.

"Who?" Sandra asked.

I shrugged, not wanting to upset Sandra with the story of our Charlottetown adventure. When Sherry returned everyone ordered lobster except me. "I'll try the steak and potatoes, but only if they're the famous PEI potatoes."

"I guarantee that, Madam."

As she left Sandra laughed. "Madam! She must think you're a senior citizen in disguise, Liz, or else just plain weird."

Ignoring the others' giggles I clapped along to a toe-tapper on the organ requested by someone from North Carolina, and then played peek-a-boo with a blond baby in a nearby high chair. When Sherry appeared with our plates my mouth started to water.

"The lobster looks fabulous, and you even get melted butter to dip it in. I made a big mistake ordering steak."

Katie smiled as she knotted a bib around her neck. "You can try a small piece of mine, Liz."

"Great, but let's be fair. You can have all my turnips."

I was impressed with my coach's skill as she twisted off a claw and cracked it open to dig out the meat with a thin fork. "Oh my," she said, rolling her eyes, "is it ever good."

"That poor little lobster was scuttling around the ocean floor just yesterday without a care in the world, probably listening to its Walkman and planning a day at the beach. Instead, you're tearing it to shreds. Sandra, how could you?"

She looked at my steak. "And that was a cow peacefully chewing its cud under the sun." Smiling, she gave me some lobster and then looked at Makiko. "How's yours?"

"So nice! Japanese eat lobster tail raw with soya and *wasabi*, but cooked also good." She turned to me. "When visit Japan we travel on famous bullet train. At each station is served *ekiben*, lunch in box. Fish and vegetable and rice with sour plum. Is very delicious."

I laughed. "No, is very toothsome." Chewing the lobster I studied the crowd and then saw a beautiful redhead standing by the entrance. "Hey, there's Breanne. Maybe she'd like to join us."

I waved but she didn't see me across the crowded room. When the hostess approached with a menu Breanne shook her head, then bit a fingernail as she stared at the organist. I decided she was waiting for her husband to park their car, but something strange happened. The bearded man with the ripped T-shirt left his table to say something to Breanne. She nodded and they headed outside.

"I'll be right back," I said.

"Liz!" Sandra exclaimed. "What's going on?"

"Tell you in a minute."

The moment I reached the parking lot I spotted Breanne and the bearded man. They were standing beside a car that looked familiar—maybe because every second person on the island seemed to drive that make. At first I thought it was hers, then realized it was so dirty it had to be the man's car. As if to prove me right he reached in the open window for something that glittered in the sunlight.

It was a long hypodermic needle.

The thing was so scary I stepped back against the church wall. The man said something, and Breanne shook her head angrily. Just then, the door of the nearby house opened and a priest with snowy hair and glasses stepped out. Beside him was a golden lab, which bounded across the parking lot to greet Breanne and the man. When they ignored the dog it continued on to me, and I knelt to rub its head.

The priest smiled as he approached. "I can tell Belle likes you." He asked where I was from, then said he was a great fan of Winnipeg's hockey team. As we talked I heard the squeal of rubber and saw Breanne tearing out of the parking lot in a fancy sports car. Seconds later the bearded man followed in his filthy car.

"He's got a real oil-burner there," the priest said, watching the car lurch away past the green fields. "People should take better care of their belongings."

"You certainly take good care of Belle. She's a beauty."

"Thanks young lady." The priest held the door for me as we went back inside. "Enjoy your lobster but leave room for dessert!"

This was good advice—the others were already digging into strawberry shortcake when I reached the table. "This is real whipped cream," Katie said, giving me a sample while I waited for Sherry to take my order. Then I leaned toward the others to tell them what I'd seen.

"A needle?" Sandra said. "Aren't they used by people who take heroin?"

"Exactly what I thought! That guy in the ripped T-shirt looked like a drug pusher to me."

"But *Breanne*? Surely . . . ?"

"I know it's weird but that's what I saw. Should we call the police?"

As Sandra hesitated her sister said, "Absolutely not. There's no proof of anything. Needles are also used in medicine. Maybe that man's a doctor."

"A slob like him?"

"He should wear a white uniform to eat lobster?"

Sandra nodded. "She's right. You'd better drop it. Liz."

I glanced at Makiko but she was too polite to disagree with them, so I ate my dessert in gloomy silence. Then something happened outside the church that made me even sorrier for myself. As we were heading across the parking lot I recognized Sabrina, the woman in sandals who called herself a princess, just getting out of a car. With her was a mean-looking man in a leather jacket who Sabrina introduced as her brother. There was a tense moment when she demanded that I pay her the twenty-dollar bet she claimed I owed her for not guessing her age, but I just walked away, and nothing more was said. This sure didn't improve my mood, and I got into Katie's car feeling melancholy and frustrated.

I knew I'd witnessed *something* important at Saint Ann's but what? It drove me crazy to be so close to the truth and yet not have the answer.

* * *

The sunshine was so hot the next day that I asked Alvin to break eggs on his pickup, just to see if they'd cook. When he didn't go for the idea Eleanor suggested boiling eggs on the stove instead—for a picnic at the beach. That sounded like a great idea so I phoned Makiko and Aaron to arrange a meeting place.

The picnic basket was heavy so I loaded it onto the farm's bicycle and pedalled to Cavendish through the heat waves rising from the road. North of town I spotted the grassy dunes standing above the beach like a series of giant heads with shaggy green hair looking out to sea. The salty smell of the ocean tickled my nose as I hauled the bicycle up some wooden stairs and over the dunes.

The wide beach was crowded and yet seemed empty because it was so long. I couldn't even see the end when I looked in each direction. The sea was a vivid blue, stretching to the flat horizon where two ships looked ready to fall over the edge. More than ready for a swim, I spread the blanket and then turned around just as Aaron appeared over the dunes.

"Fabulous place! You're so lucky to live here."

He laughed. "Maybe, but you sure improve the scenery."

"Golden words," I said, trying not to grin. "I hope Makiko gets here soon. Her father's driving her over."

"Lucky girl. I'd hate to think of Shaw's Hotel making her ride a bicycle like that."

I smiled at my bike, which was covered with fluorescent paint in strange designs. "Unique, eh? One of the boys at the farm did that for a Canada Day parade. I forgot to ask if he won a ribbon."

We charged across the hot sand and dove into the heart of a breaker. For a moment there was bubbly silence and then I broke the surface, shaking the salt water out of my eyes as I grinned at Aaron. "This is so great," I yelled, plunging under again to swim and swim until my lungs were bursting. Then I floated on the surface with my face to the sun, thinking I'd never been happier.

Makiko joined us soon after and we stayed in the ocean for a long time, eventually emerging with wrinkled skin and blue lips. As we towelled off I spotted a tiny creature hopping across the sand and bent to examine it.

"That's a beach-hopper," Aaron said. "It must be hungry. Mostly they hide in the sand until dark."

"Does it want our picnic?"

"Nope, just some tasty seaweed. Crazy, huh?"

Makiko smiled. "In Japan seaweed favourite food. Make long life, fine health."

"So I've heard, but hamburgers smell much better." Opening the basket he sniffed like a cat. "It smells good, but where's the sizzle of frying burgers?"

Laughing, I laid out the feast Eleanor had made for us, and soon we were munching our way though a luscious picnic. "You know," Aaron said between bites, "the sea looks empty and yet there's so much life out there. Once I put my finger in the mouth of a jellyfish and let it bite me."

"Did it hurt?"

He shook his head. "They're neat things, you know. If they get broken apart each section becomes a new jelly fish, just like in those old monster movies where the blob threatens to multiply and take over the world." He smiled and continued in a dramatic voice, "And only Austen the Great can save civilization."

Makiko laughed. "Is true! Austen-san will solve riddle of Green Gables."

"We'll do it together!" I said, then glanced shyly at Aaron. "Maybe you'd like to help, too?"

"You bet I'd like." Polishing off a huge piece of chocolate cake, Aaron leaned back with a sigh. "You know my favourite food? Oysters. You crack open the shell and slurp them down your throat like a raw egg."

"Yeccch!"

"Just you wait Liz, and I'll get you eating them." Shielding his eyes against the sun he looked out to sea. "It's hard to imagine a terrible storm off this shore, isn't it? But it sure can get bad around here when the weather breaks. A long time ago hundreds of American fishermen were trapped in their little boats by a storm that lasted almost fifty hours. A lot of men drowned."

"This actually happened?"

"Yup, but want to hear something really creepy? A guy came up here to claim the bodies of his sons and put them aboard a schooner bound for Maine. The captain was supposed to wait for good weather but he was so angry about all the deaths that he challenged the sea to do its worst. The schooner set sail and was never seen again."

I rubbed my arms. "This island has too many ghost stories." When I described our experience at the kirk Aaron nodded.

"It's quite a church. Our choir's singing there tomorrow night at a special service. Care to come?"

"Sure, but the timing's wrong. We're going to the musical."

"Then how about meeting afterwards at the Queen Street mall? I'll buy you both a double chocolate milkshake, and maybe a hamburger, too."

"Sounds great." I let red sand run through my fingers, then watched some people down the beach rigging up a volleyball net. When a serve went bouncing away I stared in dismay as the ball rolled to a stop near a familiar figure.

"It's that ump again. He keeps showing up to rain on my parade."

"My . . . Mr. Lodge isn't such a bad guy."

"Want a bet? He kicked me out of the game."

Aaron smiled. "You're cute when you're sulking."

"But what's that guy doing? He's stopping at every group on the beach. Some people are shaking their heads, but others are nodding."

"Yes," Makiko said, "and please to notice, Austen-san. Some give money to wicked ump."

"I wish I'd brought binoculars. What's he handing those people?"

Aaron smiled. "Do you see criminals everywhere? He's probably just selling tickets to his museum about Maud. The guy's a real hustler. You've got to give him credit."

Makiko looked at Aaron. "Is museum in countryside?"

He nodded. "It's out the coast road, just past Jake's Store."

"Museum is found on top floor of house occupied by wicked ump?"

"That's the one. Have you been there?"

"Yes," Makiko said. Then she added shyly, "Is not good museum. Very disappointing. A chair where famous Maud perhaps sat, and a pen possibly hers. Most disappointing. Not like birthplace, where I see silver tea service actual wedding gift, or Park Corner where man show me patchwork quilt of Maud."

"He keeps searching for authentic stuff but it's all been snapped up. You know that typewriter at Green

Gables, the one Maud wrote her books on? He keeps asking for it, because then his museum would be a big success, but the government always refuses. It's not fair when they don't need the typewriter to get people into Green Gables."

"I wonder what's going to happen there?" I said. "It's closed because of the police investigation but do you think it'll reopen? Maybe the government won't want a bunch of ghouls staring at the room where Miss Martin died."

Makiko nodded. "Then typewriter can go to wicked ump?"

"Could be." I watched the umpire as he moved slowly down the beach away from us. "That guy bothers me. What could he be selling those people?"

Makiko laughed. "Heroin!"

"Probably not, but I'd sure like to learn more about him. Like, if he was still at Green Gables when Miss Martin was murdered."

9

The musical was a marvellous experience.

Humphrey escorted me to a place in the darkened wings near the actors waiting to make their entrance, but where I could also see the action on stage. The only disappointment was that Sandra couldn't make it.

"How is she?" Humphrey whispered.

I looked at the concern in his blue eyes, hoping this meant Cupid's arrows had hit their target. "I'm sure it's only a twenty-four-hour flu. Tomorrow she'll be right as rain."

"I hope so because we've got a date. I'm taking her to visit a place called Sea Cow Cove. Sandra loves that name!"

"She's a *fabulous* person, Humphrey, and I mean that."

He laughed. "Would I doubt you?"

As he began turning the handle of a strange machine the lights came up on stage and I saw Matthew in a buggy with Anne. While she sang to the audience Matthew cracked a whip and called *giddyup!* but there wasn't a horse, just Humphrey cranking in the rope which was pulling the buggy across the stage. When it reached the wings he helped Anne down and she hurried with Matthew to a false-fronted house.

"That's Green Gables," Humphrey whispered. "Neat, eh?"

Leaning forward, I watched the action with wide eyes. I couldn't see the audience but I heard chuckles when Anne signed off her prayers with "Yours respectfully." Then there was a roar of laughter when a nasty woman booted a cradle to quiet her crying baby. I joined in even though she seemed horrible, but moments later the woman came into the wings and surprised me with a warm smile. "Know something?" I whispered to Humphrey. "It's confusing being around actors. They can hide their true selves behind any disguise."

There was a lot of dancing in the show, so it was fun watching dancers warm up offstage with stretches and high kicks, but the best thing was talking to the kids waiting for the schoolhouse scene. A girl with a purple bow in her long hair learned I'd been at Green Gables and told me everyone was gossiping about A.P. Cole's mysterious disappearance.

"Nobody that gorgeous could get ill," she giggled. "I think he's run away with someone rich."

A boy leaned close to whisper, "Who murdered Miss Martin?"

I shrugged. "A lot of people were in the house that night. One of them had to be responsible."

At that moment someone tapped my shoulder and I looked up at 'Cameron of the Yard'—only it was no longer him. The actor still had a meaty face but the big moustache was gone and so were the thick eyebrows. He'd been transformed by some kind of magic into a bald farmer with a hoe and a straw hat. "Enjoying yourself?" he asked, then grabbed a slingshot from the boy's pocket and aimed it at me, grinning.

I flinched. "You shouldn't point weapons," I said, trying to smile. "My Dad's a police officer and he's always telling me that."

He stared at me for a moment, then walked away. Soon after, he was on stage with the whole cast, singing and dancing in a big picnic scene. As the curtain fell there was a wave of applause from the audience, then excited chatter as people headed into the lobby for the intermission. I was going to join Makiko and Mr. Tanaka but Humphrey invited me to come and chat with the actors.

There was a babble of conversation from cast members standing around in a long hallway, while others sat in the various dressing rooms. I felt kind of shy, but Humphrey introduced me to some of the people I didn't know, and others gave me pleasant waves.

"I remember you from Green Gables," said the man who played Matthew. "That was a shocking night. I can't say Miss Martin was friendly with the rest of us in the musical, but she was a hard worker." He leaned toward a mirror surrounded by light bulbs to check his makeup. "I've got her cat now."

"Wow! The Siamese?"

"Yup. I heard an ad on the radio and hurried over to that gal's apartment. The kitty's settled in very nicely with me."

"Oh, what a relief! My folks said I'd already brought home enough strays so I've been worried for it."

Matthew started to reply, then suddenly fell silent. So did everyone else and at first I wondered if I'd said something terrible, but they were all turned toward the hallway. From somewhere I heard whistling, followed by a loud *ssssh!* and then a furious discussion carried on in low voices. I had no idea what was happening. Then Humphrey hurried into the hallway so I followed him.

'Cameron of the Yard' stood outside a small dressing room, so angry his face was beet red. As he stomped away I went forward and saw Breanne in the dressing room. There were tears in her eyes.

"I didn't know," she said to Humphrey. "I'd never heard."

"Don't worry, Breanne. Theatre people are extremely s-s-superstitious."

"What happened?" I asked.

"Actors never whistle in a dressing room. They s-s-say it will bring calamity. It's bad enough what happened to Miss Martin, we don't want disaster for anyone else."

Breanne looked at me. "I'm a professional singer, not an actress. This is my first stage role, so I've never heard that superstition. I've been really nervous and was just trying to cheer myself up."

I tried to smile. "Don't worry about it. Everything will be fine."

Over the loudspeaker a voice announced *three minutes, ladies and gentlemen.* As Breanne quickly repaired the damage to her eye make-up and left the dressing room, Humphrey picked up a container of salt from the dressing table.

"S-s-some actors put s-s-salt on their tongues to loosen their voices for s-s-singing." As he returned the container to the table he fumbled and it fell to the floor. I stared in horror as white crystals spilled out, then quickly knelt down.

"Help me, Humphrey! Toss some over your left shoulder." Three times I pinched salt between my fingers to throw over my shoulder, then Humphrey dropped down beside me and did the same. "Whistling and now salt," I groaned. "This is horrible."

"Only if you're s-s-superstitious."

"Maybe you're not, but I sure am."

"Better make s-s-sure the lid is closed. Let's not have another accident."

Under the container on the table was a note with lettering so large I couldn't help reading it as I checked the lid: *Good horse came ashore today at North Lake.* "Humphrey, what's the port for tuna fishing?"

"A place called North Lake. Why?"

"Oh, it's nothing."

Puzzled and upset, I hurried with Humphrey to the wings. Although the musical resumed with a neat song by the kids about their summer holidays I could hardly concentrate. Eventually Humphrey whispered, "Feeling blue? I'll tell you how s-s-some guys cheered me up when I was an actor in Toronto. I came off s-s-stage and had fifteen s-s-seconds to change into an army outfit with big boots. But they'd filled them with water and I had to s-s-slosh back out to s-s-sing while a big puddle grew around me."

I laughed. "And you're going to pull a trick on me if I don't cheer up? Okay, I promise not to worry." Moving closer to the stage I tapped my foot to a great song and then grinned as Katie brilliantly acted the scene of Diana Barry getting drunk by mistake on raspberry cordial. The audience laughed hysterically as she licked cordial off the tablecloth and then put her feet on the table to drain the bottle—just as the ladies of Avonlea walked in.

I was thrilled to hear the huge burst of applause for Katie when the musical ended and the cast took its bows. "If only Sandra had been here," I said to Humphrey, and drifted into a fantasy about being an actress myself. Waves of applause and hysterical cries of *bravo!* washed over me as I was presented with roses by the star with laryngitis I'd replaced at the last second, then again I sang Anne's show-stopping number before being surrounded by adoring fans clutching autograph books.

Humphrey nudged me. "Come on, beautiful dreamer. I promised to escort you to the mall."

"It's been a fabulous evening! I can't thank you enough."

He smiled. "The pleasure's all mine, Liz Austen. You've added s-s-some fun to my life."

"Why not move to Winnipeg? I bet Sandra wouldn't mind."

"Well, you never know what might happen." He winked. "But not a word to her."

"Believe me, your secret's safe!"

I was desperate to tell Makiko the news but a promise was a promise so I could only daydream about Sandra's blissful face when she received her diamond ring. "Wasn't it *incredible?*" I exclaimed when Makiko and her father arrived at the mall. I began to tell them all the backstage details, but every time I looked at Mr. Tanaka all I could think about was the note in Breanne's dressing room. It really upset me, so I was secretly happy when he left for Shaw's Hotel after Humphrey volunteered to drive us home.

Makiko had accepted my invitation to sleep over at Parkview Farm so we talked about that and sipped ice-cold chocolate sodas, until Aaron finally arrived from the church service. Unfortunately, Sabrina, the princess in sandals, had invited herself along. She didn't mention the twenty-dollar bet but she still spoiled the evening by talking nonstop about her childhood in Ontario until Humphrey cut her off.

"Very interesting I'm s-s-sure, Miss S-S-Sabrina, but I'd like to ask Liz about detective work." He turned to me. "I need your advice. Do you think I sh-sh-should tell the police about a blackened s-s-spoon I noticed in A.P. Cole's locker backstage?"

"I think so! My Dad told me drug addicts heat heroin in a spoon over a candle."

"S-s-so I understand."

"There's another word for heroin," I said, trying to avoid Makiko's eyes. "Horse."

Sabrina stood up abruptly. "Good night, everyone."

"Hey," Aaron said. "You haven't finished your food."

She smiled at me. "Why don't you have it, dear? It might help your figure."

Her nasty remark really hurt but I tried to forget it as Breanne approached with her husband. Sitting down, they smiled happily at our congratulations on Breanne's performance. "Notice my eyes match tonight?" she asked me. "I found the missing contact lens." Producing a small case with a pretty design on its lid she snapped it open to reveal a pair of tiny blue lenses. "But I brought along my extras just in case. I couldn't have performed Marilla blind, although maybe I wouldn't have been so nervous if I couldn't have seen the audience!"

"With respect to Miss Martin's memory," Humphrey said, "I must s-s-say you outclassed her as Marilla." As Breanne beamed he looked at me. "If only you could s-s-solve that murder, Liz."

"Is that true Humphrey, or do you still think I need my brother's help?"

"I feel guilty about my remarks. I was wrong about you."

"Thanks!" Encouraged by this, I thought yet again about Miss Martin's death. "You know," I said to Makiko, "we've never been back to Green Gables to check it out."

"Police have searched house bottom to top."

"Sure, but what about *outside*? Maybe the killer dropped something in the grass or somewhere in the woods. You know my Dad's a police officer? My parents phoned today and he told me about a case that's just been solved, only because someone found a tiny nail in a flower bed. That's what gave me the idea." I started to get really excited. "You know what? I feel like going there tonight to have a look. I can't wait until tomorrow!"

"What of darkness?"

"No sweat. We'll have each other's company." I turned to Aaron. "Want to come?"

"Sure, but what'll we look for?"

"I'm not sure. Maybe a wallet or something even smaller." I turned to Humphrey. "Do you want to come too?"

"I can't. S-s-sorry. I've s-s-still got work to do backstage." He looked at Breanne. "Would you drop the kids at Cavendish on your way home?"

"Certainly," she said, then turned to me with a frown. "I think your idea's crazy. At least wait until morning." When I didn't reply she shook her head. "Very well, but you may be asking for real trouble."

* * *

I could never have crossed the cemetery alone. The tombstones were shadowed in the moonlight and strange cries sounded from hidden creatures as we approached the woods. "This is terrifying," I whispered. "Thank goodness you came with us."

"No problem," Aaron said. "I'm only having a minor heart attack."

"Liz-san, I have great fear."

I stared at Makiko. "You've changed my name!"

She nodded. "Friendship grows strong."

"Will you ever call me plain old Liz?"

"It is hoped, but only when we truly kindred spirits."

I looked at the dark woods. "If we survive this we'll really have a lifelong bond." I glanced at the old shack as we left the cemetery and the trees closed around us. The night sounds were eerie as we cautiously followed the path into darkness, then looked at each other with huge eyes.

"Are we totally crazy?" I whispered. "Should we quit?"

"Yes, we're crazy," Aaron replied. "No, we're not quitting."

I kept looking over my shoulder, and nearly jumped out of my skin when a stick cracked under Aaron's foot. "Remember how Anne thought these woods were haunted? She said a lady walks at night, wringing her hands and wailing, just before a death in the family."

"Please Liz-san, not to have reminder at this time."

"And there's a headless man and skeletons." I shivered. "What if we meet the ghost of Miss Martin?"

"Cut it out," Aaron croaked.

"Sorry."

At last the trees thinned out and we saw moonlight ahead, spilling across the house. I almost expected to see Anne signalling to Diana from her bedroom window as we climbed the slope toward Green Gables, then Makiko grabbed my arm.

"Danger!"

Staring at the house, I saw a dim shape slip around a corner into hiding. "Who's there?" I called. "We see you!"

"What'll we do now?" Aaron whispered.

I took a deep breath. "Press on."

Makiko nodded. *"Ganbatte."*

Huddled close together we crossed the lawn to peer around the corner of the house. "What about the well?"

I whispered. "That's a hiding place we'd better check." I shook the flashlight we'd just borrowed from Parkview Farm, wishing the batteries were stronger. Following the feeble yellow glow we cautiously approached the well and looked inside.

"Nothing," Aaron said. "What now?"

I looked at Green Gables. "Do you think that person's inside?"

"I doubt it. The special alarms would have been triggered."

"So who was that?"

"A thrill seeker?"

"Maybe, maybe not." I stared at the dark trees and bushes, knowing that anyone could be watching. "Let's do our search, then get out of here." Slowly we wandered around with our eyes on the lawn until I called a halt. "This isn't working, let's use our brainpower. If the killer dropped something it must have fallen where the police couldn't see it."

"In the well?" Aaron suggested.

Returning to it, he climbed over the side. The well was only a fake so there was just a short drop to an iron-mesh grill. Aaron examined it carefully with the flashlight, but found nothing. "Okay," I said as we helped him climb out, "what now?"

"Liz-san, I have theory. I am certain Mounties search all places but bodies of police are large. We are small. Can there be place to search where only small body can fit?"

"Good thinking, Makiko." I ran the flashlight's feeble glow over the house. "Nothing at the back. Let's try the other side."

Thick bushes with thorns grew near the front door. When I got scratched trying to push them aside Makiko knelt down. “I am smallest person so I crawl under bush.”

“Be careful.”

“Not to sweat.”

Makiko wriggled into the tiny space. When she’d disappeared I glanced nervously at the dark trees, wondering if we were being watched. I heard Makiko muttering angrily at the flashlight and then, seconds later, a cry.

“Liz-san! Is something caught in branches. Please to shake bushes.”

Aaron put his foot against a thick branch and rocked it hard. A minute later Makiko crawled out covered in dirt. Her face was radiant.

“Is clue! I have feeling of certainty.” In her hand was a small plastic container. “Black colour make it invisible in bushes. But flashlight reflect on silver letter.”

“It looks like an L. Maybe it’s someone’s initial.”

“That’s a contact lens case,” Aaron said. “Let’s open it.”

Inside were two hollow spaces marked *left* and *right*. I thought it was empty until the flashlight beam glinted against the tiny lenses nestled in each hollow. “Look!” I exclaimed. “Here’s the name of the company that made them and there’s a serial number, too. I bet that company can tell the police who owns the lenses!”

“That’s true,” Aaron said, “but maybe some tourist dropped the case. It could have been here for years.”

“But there’s no dust on it.” I grinned at Makiko. “Good work!”

"Is only . . ."

She hesitated as powerful lights swept the night. Turning toward the road we saw the glare of high beams, then a door slammed. "Liz," a voice called. "Are you there?"

"We sure are, Alvin! Makiko just found a contact lens case. It's got an optician's address inside with a serial number, so the Mounties will be able to trace the owner. Isn't that great?"

"Sure, but it's really late." Alvin appeared in the headlights, waving his hand. "Come along. You can take the case to the police tomorrow but now you're going to bed. We shouldn't have let you come over here when you borrowed that flashlight."

"But it was worth it," I said as we hurried toward his pickup. "What we just found will change everything!"

10

Instead of being excited the next morning, I awoke with a sense of foreboding. I should have been pleased to learn the PEI softball team had won the championship game the night before but the fear was so strong I couldn't shake it. Even while I was out in the barn watching a new-born calf get a bath from its mother's big tongue, the feeling stayed with me and I couldn't enjoy myself.

Because of the calf Alvin wanted to stay at the farm. Eleanor was going to visit friends, so I phoned my coach. "You're the only person who can help," I told her. "We need a drive to the city."

"Humphrey's arriving soon for our trip. It's a long way to Sea Cow Cave, but I'll ask him to drive you when we return."

"Actually," I said, "that might work perfectly. Makiko's father just called to suggest we go on a boat ride. There's a charter sailing this morning from near their hotel."

I arranged to meet them later, then asked Eleanor to drop us at the hotel on her way to her friends' farm. We arrived early so there was time to enjoy the walk to the boat at Covehead Harbour. Looking up at a huge, old tree I saw a quick flash of yellow.

"Look at that canary! I wonder if it's tame?" As I made a sweet sound with my lips the canary answered with a piercing cry, hopping from branch to branch. Then it flew off into the sunshine and all my fears returned. "It's so nice being with you, Makiko. I wish you'd never go home to Japan."

She smiled. "My heart also heavy. But much time of friendship remains to us."

"I just hope that's true."

The road was deserted. To one side we saw empty dunes and, to the other, a narrow arm of the sea wandering past marshes where motionless blue herons waited for their prey to swim past. Before long a collection of small wooden buildings appeared ahead, clustered around a couple of docks. Lobster traps were stacked everywhere and I could smell hamburgers being cooked for tourists waiting to board the charter boat. For a few minutes we leaned over a bridge watching ourselves in the water, then a gull swooped down to shatter the reflection and I grabbed Makiko's arm. "Come on," I said, not wanting to tell her the broken image could mean danger for us.

We bought tickets from a boy our age with black hair

and long lashes over marvellous eyes. I thought he was wonderful until I noticed he'd short-changed me and returned angrily to the booth. "Sorry," he said. "I can't do subtracting too good. I love the sea but not this dumb summer job selling tickets. I thought I'd be out on the boats, having fun with cute tourists like you."

Immediately I forgave him everything. We had a nice talk and then I crossed the dock to join Makiko and the other people who'd boarded the boat and were sitting on the sunny deck. As I was taking Makiko's picture I saw the boy hurrying our way.

"Phone message," he said to Makiko. "You gotta return to Shaw's Hotel."

"Now?"

"Yeah. The guy said right away."

"Is my father." Makiko shook her head. "How much I wanted sea trip."

"Can't you wait? We'll be back in a couple of hours."

"I must obey wishes of father."

"I'll go with you," I said, standing up.

"No Liz-san, no no. You are on boat. Why miss golden chance? If possible I am at dock to greet your return."

Uncertain what to do, I watched her climb to the dock. The boat's lines were released and it chugged under the bridge towards the open sea. Makiko waved and I grinned, but that message had me worried. Why would her father call her home like that? But it was too late now to suggest she phone just to make sure, so I turned my face to the sea and tried to enjoy the ride.

The wind was cold despite the brilliant sunshine. I stared at the waves splashing away from the hull, then turned for a final look at the small lighthouse and red sand of Covehead Harbour. Somewhere behind the dunes Makiko was walking home along the deserted road: now I wished desperately that I'd been thinking a little bit faster when that message arrived.

"Attention folks," the young captain said, "we'll be dropping the fishing lines soon." He looked out to sea. "Enjoy the sunshine while it lasts, though, because we'll have fog by tonight. That cold wind you feel will bring it in from offshore."

"Hey," shouted the woman next to me. "Smoke!"

The captain lifted a hatch and black clouds poured out. "No problem folks, it's just a minor malfunction." He killed the engine and, with a fire extinguisher close at hand, spent several minutes tinkering. Then he shook his head. "I'll have to radio to Covehead. Another boat will tow us home."

The tourists groaned but my heart leapt with joy. Anxiously I watched the shore and finally saw white waves foaming away from a boat as it came our way. "Faster," I muttered, "put the boots to it." At last the rescuer threw a line to our captain and we began the journey to Covehead Harbour. The boy who'd brought Makiko the message was watching from the dock. "I'm worried about my friend," I told him the moment I left the boat. "Can we phone the hotel to see if Makiko arrived safely?"

"Sure, but her name isn't Makiko."

"What do you mean?"

He produced a scrap of paper from his pocket. "Look, her name's Liz. I wrote it down." The paper said *Liz—blak hair & iyes.* "That's the description the man gave over the phone."

"He asked for Liz? Then why'd you give the message to Makiko?"

"She's got black hair and eyes."

"So do I! Don't you understand? It was *me* the caller wanted!"

He shrugged. "My job's selling tickets, not running a message service." I watched him walk away, then raced to the bridge. Shielding my eyes I looked down the road, and saw nothing but emptiness.

* * *

My worst fears were confirmed when I phoned the hotel; they hadn't seen Makiko since we'd left together that morning. "Something's happened to her! Phone the police right away!"

By the time I ran back to the hotel, the place was swarming with Mounties. I told them everything about the message and the mistaken identity, and then produced the contact lens case. The blond officer who'd investigated at Green Gables agreed it could be important but wasn't sure the initial was an I. "It depends how you look at it," she said. "Try turning the case and . . ."

The office door crashed open and I saw Mr. Tanaka. He looked terrible. "My daughter! Is she safe?"

"I'm sure we'll find her, sir. Please sit down."

He slumped into a chair. "I have driven here so rapidly from North Lake. All the way my heart says *this cannot be!*" He buried his face in his hands, then stared at the Mountie. "I will pay money! Whatever is demanded."

Next through the door were Alvin and my coach.

"We drove straight over," Sandra exclaimed. "Alvin caught me before Humphrey arrived. We're taking you straight back to the farm."

I tried to smile. "You're almost hysterical, coach. I'm worried your hair will turn white."

"What would your parents have said if *you* were missing!"

They rushed me to the pickup and we drove home in silence, each of us deeply worried about Makiko. At the farm Eleanor wrapped a hug around me, and the boys hovered so close I finally threw my hands in the air. "Hey guys, I don't need a bodyguard inside your kitchen!"

They stepped back a few paces but remained watchful. The atmosphere was tense as we tried to eat supper, then gazed sadly at the TV news reports about Makiko's disappearance. Friends and neighbours kept phoning the MacNeills, then Alvin waved me over. "This call's for you."

The muffled voice made the hairs on my neck stand up. "Liz Austen," the caller said with that distinctive PEI accent, "listen carefully. If you want to see Makiko alive again, be at the Boardwalk at 9 p.m. Be alone and do not contact the police."

* * *

Shortly before nine I rode the fluorescent bicycle down the farm road and headed for Cavendish. I could smell the fog predicted by the tour boat captain, and saw it rolling in towards shore. It was really spooky, but I was determined not to let anything stop me. After the cemetery I passed the local amusement park with its flying saucer, then King Tut's Tomb and the Enchanted Castle. The last of the tourist attractions was the Boardwalk, a row of wooden stores where tourists could buy souvenirs and T-shirts and food.

I locked the bike to a tree behind the stores, then joined the tourists wandering around. Finally I went into Cows, a place I'd heard was famous for its homemade ice cream. Pretty red lampshades hung from the ceiling and a ceramic cow gazed at me from the counter as I waited my turn.

"Next please," said a girl with brown pigtails.

"I'd like a double butter-brickle cone," I said, "plus a scoop of chocolate chip."

She smiled. "Feeling hungry?"

"No, scared."

"What's wrong?"

"Nothing. I was just kidding."

The cone was delicious but I really wasn't very hungry. Going outside, I studied the faces around me without recognizing anyone—until a man approached. I remembered his black leather jacket and his mean eyes from our first meeting outside Saint Ann's Church: he was supposedly Sabrina's brother.

"Hey you," he said, stepping in front of me. "My sister wants a word."

"How about rude? That's a good word for her."

"Funny, funny." He gestured at a parking lot on the far side of a patch of grass. "She's waiting in the car."

As he started toward it I hesitated, then realized I had to follow for Makiko's sake. Dumping my cone into a litter bin, I walked nervously across the lawn to the beat-up old car.

Sabrina rolled down her window as I came near. "Where's my twenty bucks?" she demanded.

"What are you talking about?"

"You lost that bet when you couldn't guess my age. I want the money you owe me."

"I never had a chance to answer. Otherwise I'd have said you're eighty-two, and I'd have won the bet."

"Get in the car," Sabrina said angrily, "and we'll talk real serious about money."

"No way."

I started to back away, but her brother grabbed my arm. "Do what Sabrina says," he ordered, shoving me toward the car.

"Leave me alone!"

As I tried to wrench free I saw a woman with a baby carriage staring at me. Suddenly she pulled a gun out of hiding, aimed it at Sabrina's brother and yelled, "Freeze!" At the same moment another woman leapt from a parked car and several men raced our way, producing revolvers from under beach clothes and from inside a camera case. Sabrina's brother stared at them in stunned silence, then was whirled around and spread-eagled against the car.

"What's going on?" he shouted.

"Police," said the blond officer I'd spoken with at Green Gables. "Don't make a move. We want to talk to you about a kidnapping."

As Sabrina was ordered out of the car and also frisked for weapons she turned to me. "Tell them you know us!"

I stared at her silently.

"Come on," Sabrina pleaded. "We're not kidnappers. Tell them!"

A crowd was rapidly gathering. They whispered excitedly as handcuffs were slapped on Sabrina's wrists, then her brother's. There was real fear in their eyes but I didn't say a word until Sabrina blurted, "Come on, help us! I'll forget the twenty bucks."

Turning to the officer I said, "It's okay. I don't think they're involved in Makiko's kidnapping."

Sabrina looked relieved until the officer shook her head. "We'll still take them in for questioning." As the two were bundled into a police car, protesting loudly, the officer looked worried. "If they aren't involved, we're in trouble. Our cover is blown, and the person who phoned the farm will have seen all this. We'd better get you back home."

"What about Makiko? What happens now?"

"We'll hope for the best, and follow all leads."

"But every second counts!" I looked at my watch, thinking fast, then turned to the officer. "Can you wait for me? I'd like to get another cone."

She smiled. "You've got a bigger appetite than my son. Okay, but make it fast."

Pushing through the crowd, I raced to Cows. Because of the commotion outside there were no customers at the counter. Hurrying to the girl in pigtails I whispered, "Some creep is following me. Can I sneak away through the back?"

Seconds later I ran out through a screen door. With shaking hands I unlocked my bike and wheeled it toward the nearby woods. Within minutes I was zooming along a path through the trees, then across a field where wisps of fog were gathering around tall stands of wild lupines. The fog had arrived quickly, muffling the world in total silence.

I followed the path to a second field, then finally reached the coast road. Praying I was heading in the right direction I pedalled through the darkness until I saw a small neon sign ahead. Slowly it grew larger, then I passed Jake's Store and, soon after, I saw the sign at the end of a country lane that I'd been looking for. I ditched the bike in some bushes and walked slowly down the lane, trying to see through the fog. Somewhere in the night a dog barked, but the rest of the world was silent.

At last I saw a light burning over a porch. Moving closer, I made out the shape of a wooden house. It looked empty, until a light went on upstairs and I saw someone's shadow against a curtain. Hoping no sticks would crack under my feet I went closer, thinking I could look in a window.

But the curtains were pulled everywhere. As I stared unhappily at the house I felt a cat rubbing against my leg and bent to stroke it. Just then, a second tabby appeared through a basement window that had been propped open. As the cats disappeared into the night I opened the window wider and looked into the dark basement.

If I wanted to get to Makiko, I had to take the chance.

Wiggling through the window I quietly lowered myself to the floor. Around me were dim shapes of cartons and shelves. The only sound was my own harsh breathing, until I heard footsteps directly above. The next sound was a faint voice that seemed female.

Reaching out a blind hand, I felt my way forward between the cartons. I had to find stairs to get close enough to identify the voice. If it was Makiko's I could get the police here quickly, but first I needed proof. As something sticky touched my face I wiped it away, then realized it was a cobweb. At the same moment I felt something run across my skin. A spider! A shriek erupted from my mouth before I could stop it. I froze. My heart was pounding.

Had I been heard? Dropping to my knees, I crawled behind a carton. Footsteps crossed the floor, a door opened and light spilled down some wooden stairs. Feet appeared, then a man came slowly down the stairs.

It was the umpire.

* * *

For a moment he stared into the darkness, then muttered something about noisy cats and returned upstairs. When the door closed I let out a long sigh. But I still had to identify that female voice. The thought of Makiko's *Ganbatte!* gave me courage and I moved towards the stairs.

They creaked as I cautiously climbed up—my eyes level with the crack of light under the door. Leaning close, I saw the umpire's feet as he moved around a kitchen table. The crackly voice of a woman said, "You are listening to CBC News," but she was silenced when the umpire clicked off his radio. For several long moments the house was quiet, then something thumped to the floor.

It was a big haversack, the kind used to haul supplies into the wilderness. I saw the umpire's hands close the drawstrings, then he pulled the canvas bag across the floor towards a hallway. *What was inside it?* I stared at the thing, until the umpire opened the front door and dragged his burden outside.

Creeping quickly down the stairs I headed for the faint outline of the window. The air outside smelled so good after the musty basement. Close by I heard the umpire's grumbles and the scuff of the haversack being hauled away into the foggy darkness. Hoping I was invisible to him, I followed the sounds for several minutes until they stopped.

For a long time there was silence, broken only by distant barking. Then I heard a spluttering sound, followed by the roar of an engine. Two lights, one red and one green, shone through the fog. As they began moving I heard the splash of waves and realized the umpire was in a boat.

He was getting away, and I was powerless to stop him.

* * *

At Jake's Store I found a pay phone on the outside wall. I called the Mounties in Charlottetown and told them what I'd just seen. The person I spoke to said an officer would meet me at Parkview Farm to get more information.

As I pedalled through the night I reviewed my evidence against the umpire. There wasn't a lot, but he did have the same accent as the man who'd phoned me at the farm, and I'd remembered him calling me a snolly-goster during the softball game, the same strange word used by the anonymous letter-writer who'd attacked Miss Martin's plans. Of course that didn't prove he'd kidnapped Makiko, but everything about him seemed so sinister.

Then I remembered the evening of the memorial service, when I'd seen the umpire come out of the woods near the shack in the cemetery. He'd been carrying something—maybe evidence from Green Gables that he wanted to hide in the cemetery.

Or in the shack.

Makiko had suggested something could be hidden there. What if the umpire had taken the haversack along the coast in his boat this evening, intending to hide it inside the shack? If I waited until I reached the farm to tell the police it might be too late to save Makiko. As I pedalled up the hill past the cemetery, I made my decision. Cutting to the right, I stopped by the arch and I leaned my bike against it.

Then I took a deep breath and entered the graveyard.

The tombstones loomed out of the darkness as I started down the slope in the direction of the shack. The fog pressed around me, cold and wet. A car passed on the road, its engine muffled and the lights fighting the grey, swirling blanket that filled the night. I was really scared, but I had to keep going.

At last I found the shack, but I'd forgotten about the lock on the door. I stared at it in dismay, then remembered with a shock that the lock we'd seen before was rusty. This one was brand new.

"Makiko?" I called softly. "Are you in there?"

When there was no reply I smashed the window with a rock and crawled inside. I stopped for a moment to let my eyes adjust to the darkness. Then I saw a blanket on the floor and the pale oval shape of a face. Makiko!

She was unconscious, but her breathing was regular. As I checked her pulse I heard voices and raised my head to listen. Then I barely had time to scramble into hiding before a key turned in the lock and the dark shape of a man entered the shack.

11

I remained silent as the man knelt beside Makiko. Moments later a second figure entered the shack and I gasped in surprise. It was Aaron!

They both turned in my direction. "Who's that?" the man said. For a brief second I considered escaping from the shack but I couldn't abandon Makiko. Standing up, I looked at Aaron.

"I can't believe it! *You* helped kidnap Makiko!"

Despite the darkness I could see his surprise. "What are you talking about? I just . . ." Then he was interrupted as the man stepped toward us. He was in a Mountie's uniform and I realized he was the person who'd first arrived at Green Gables to discover Miss Martin's body.

"We thought you'd be here," he said. "Aaron spotted

your bicycle beside the cemetery gate. Then we followed your trail through the wet grass."

Aaron nodded. "I was walking to the farm for a visit with you. I'd just seen your bike when this officer pulled up in his car. We decided to investigate in case you'd been kidnapped too."

"Well," I said, "I'm glad you're here!" Quickly I outlined my theory about the umpire bringing Makiko here, then suggested we get her to the hospital.

"A good idea," the Mountie said. "I think she'll be okay, but she's been drugged. The Charlottetown hospital's the right place for her."

He was a heavy man with strong arms so he easily lifted Makiko. Passing the tombstones I kept glancing nervously behind, fearing the umpire was lurking somewhere behind us and would leap out at any second. But nothing happened and we soon reached the Mountie's car. Like my Dad's, it had no police markings or emergency lights. I watched the man put Makiko in the back seat and cover her with the blanket from the shack, then I got into the front between him and Aaron.

"Are you going to radio headquarters about the umpire?"

The Mountie started the car. "This vehicle isn't equipped with a radio."

"Besides which," Aaron said, "you're wrong about the ump. He's not involved."

"What about the big haversack he loaded into his boat? I'm sure that's how he brought Makiko to the shack."

"Maybe there was something else in the haversack. Didn't you think of that?"

I shrugged and said nothing. For some reason Aaron seemed kind of defensive about the umpire and I sure didn't want to have him mad at me. Instead I concentrated on our progress through the fog, watching it whirl past as I thought happily about Makiko's rescue.

"You know," the Mountie said, almost like he was a mind-reader, "you deserve congratulations, young lady. Are you planning to join your father's police force some day?"

I grinned. "You never know. Detective work sure is fun."

"Your brother will be impressed with your latest success. Or maybe a bit jealous?"

The car reached a major road and picked up speed. A green sign came out of the darkness with the warning *Charlottetown Next Right*, but we kept going straight. "You missed the turn," Aaron said, then muttered angrily to himself when the man didn't reply.

"What's wrong?" I asked. "Makiko's safe, but you're still tense."

"What about the ump? You'll probably convince the police to throw him in prison."

"That'll only happen if he's guilty."

"But he's not!"

"How can you be so certain?"

"Because he's my uncle."

"*What?* Why didn't you tell me earlier?"

"Because I like you." Aaron shook his head. "You kept putting him down, and I didn't have the courage to say anything. I thought you'd turn off me."

"Aaron, I'm really sorry. That was stupid of me."

"He's not a crook Liz, and he certainly wouldn't hurt anyone. Sure he's gruff, but that's just his manner. My aunt died last year and he hasn't got over losing her. It's made him sad and angry, and I feel awful to see it."

I touched his hand. "I'm sorry."

"I'm glad I finally told you." Aaron paused, thinking. "That day at the beach he really was selling tickets to his museum. And you know that haversack? I bet it was filled with food and supplies. He's leaving around now for a week with some buddies at a cabin they've rented."

"But what about the cemetery? He came out of the woods carrying something the night of the memorial service."

"Probably wild flowers for my aunt's grave. He goes there in the evenings, after he closes his museum."

With my theory shattered I stared glumly at the passing night. If the umpire hadn't taken Makiko to the shack, who had? Now I wished there'd been time to search it for clues, or maybe find fingerprints on that shiny lock. Realizing the Mountie might have kept the lock after opening it, I was turning to ask when I heard sounds from the back seat. Makiko had opened her eyes and was trying to sit up.

"Are you okay?" I asked with a smile.

"Little bit." She rubbed her eyes. "Where please is this?"

"We're . . ."

"Lie down," the Mountie said sharply. "Don't you understand how sick you are?"

Makiko looked at him in confusion, then did as she was ordered. I was surprised by the man's tone but decided he was edgy like the rest of us. I started to ask about the lock and then slammed my mouth shut. *Where'd he get the key to open it?* I gave him a frightened look, then tried desperately to think of an escape plan. But nothing entered my mind until a phone booth appeared ahead.

"Can we stop, please?"

"Why?"

"I've got to, uh, phone someone." I hesitated. "The farm! I've got to phone Parkview Farm."

"What for?"

"The MacNeills must be terribly worried. I'm supposed to meet an officer there. If I don't arrive the Mounties will start a search."

He gave me a long look, then pulled over just past the phone booth. "I'll call the farm. Give me the map from that glove compartment."

As I pushed around some stuff inside the compartment I accidentally touched the button that popped open the car's trunk. Finding a Hertz folder with a map I passed it to the man, then waited anxiously for him to leave the car. The moment his door closed I slammed down the lock while shouting to Aaron, "Lock that door!"

"Why?"

"Because!" I looked at the shock on the man's face, then watched him dash around the front of the car. "He's not a Mountie!"

Finally Aaron reacted and got the door locked just before the man grabbed the handle. For a moment he stared at us, then disappeared in the direction of the phone booth. I couldn't see it because the trunk lid was open. Looking at Makiko I asked, "Are you okay?"

"Not so good. Perhaps better soon."

"Liz," Aaron said, "what's this all about?"

"The Mountie's a fake! This car's rented from Hertz!"

Makiko groaned so horribly that I crawled over the seat to kneel beside her. There was cold sweat on her forehead and she was trembling. As I tucked the blanket around her I said to Aaron, "How'd the Mountie get into the shack?"

"He opened the lock."

"Where'd the key come from?"

"Out of his pocket."

"You see? He's the person who locked Makiko in there."

"But why?"

"I don't know Aaron, but we're in a lot of trouble. I just hope that guy doesn't have a gun in his uniform holster."

"The car keys are in the starter."

"Great! We can . . ."

As Makiko shuddered violently and I tried to comfort her, Aaron leaned over the seat to watch anxiously. Then he said, "Some old man's walking our way. Maybe he can help us."

"What's he look like?"

"Nothing special. He's got a silver-headed cane."

"I guess it's okay. Ask him if there's a farm around here to get help." I bent over Makiko, wiping her forehead, then suddenly remembered where I'd last seen a silver-headed cane. "Aaron, keep the door locked! He was at Green Gables!"

But it was too late. A gust of cold air swirled into the car as the door opened and I turned to see a gun in the old man's hand.

* * *

Aaron was ordered to close the trunk lid, then the old man started the car and we took off into the night. "You meddler," he said angrily, looking in the mirror. "I think I'll finish you off."

"You wouldn't dare." I tried to sound brave as I stared at his heavy face and thick white hair. "Did you kill Miss Martin?"

He nodded.

"But why?"

"Don't think she didn't deserve it. It was all her fault, if only she wasn't so greedy. Years ago I was an actor in a play with Molly. One night she happened to be with me when I got into a fight with a guy outside a pub. The guy died—weak heart or something. It wasn't my fault. I went into hiding but Molly—good old Molly, my friend Molly—turned me in. But not until they'd offered a reward, I might add. I told her I'd get her for that—and I meant it." He paused, thinking. "Twenty years in prison, that's what I got, thanks to her. I only got out recently, but it sure wasn't hard to find her—the actors' union keeps track of all its members and kindly provided me with her address. Why, I even got a job working right beside her so I could figure out how I could get my revenge."

"I don't understand," Aaron said. "Why didn't she recognize you?"

The man smiled. "I told you I was an actor. They called me 'The Man of Many Faces' because I was brilliant at disguises and false identities. Still am—twenty years locked up, but I didn't forget her or the disguises. Molly never even recognized me."

"Because you were disguised as an old man?"

"No."

"Then who . . .?"

"That's for me to know, so don't waste your breath asking."

Trying to sound brave, I demanded to know where he was taking us. When the man didn't reply I stared out the window, frightened and confused. Then I remembered something. "I just realized how you killed Miss Martin! At Green Gables you went outside, saying you were ill. I bet you changed into the Mountie's uniform at your car."

"Exactly. Molly kept the Mystery Weekend plans in her Festival dressing room, so I took a good look to know exactly when she'd go upstairs and leave Matthew and Cameron to question the guests. Knowing she'd be alone, I appeared in my Mountie disguise and ordered everyone to stay downstairs. Then it was easy. I went to the bedroom where I'd earlier left the revenge note, and overpowered her. You can imagine her shock when I finally told her who I was. After I'd injected her with a lethal dose of heroin, I came back downstairs with the news of her death."

"Then you went outside and disguised yourself again as an old man?"

"Exactly. I called the police from a phone on the wall of the gift shop, and came back inside. Nobody guessed a thing. I settled back into my job, intending to stay on the island, but I'd made one mistake."

"I bet it was something about that contact lens case."

"Right again, you clever little meddler. Normally I wear clear contacts, so my disguise at work included fake eyeglasses that only had plain glass in them. As the Mountie I wore blue contacts, meaning I had to remove my clear lenses. I put them in a plastic container which I shoved into my uniform pocket. Then I made my mistake. As I approached the door of Green Gables I pulled some gloves out of my pocket, not wanting to leave fingerprints in the house. Unknown to me the plastic container fell out of my pocket and . . ."

"And into the bush where Makiko found it! So *you* were the person sneaking around that night, trying to find the case."

He nodded. "I'd looked everywhere in my car, and I'd checked my uniform pockets a hundred times, but I was stumped until you talked about the killer maybe dropping something outside Green Gables. I drove straight there, but without a flashlight I couldn't find the container. I had to get it back so the cops couldn't trace me through its serial number."

"Did you know we found the case?" Aaron asked.

"Of course. I was about to take it from you when the guy from the farm arrived in his pickup truck." He looked at me in the mirror. "The next day I learned your plans and sent a message to Covehead Harbour, hoping to grab you and maybe get the container back. I wore my Mountie disguise and waited on the roadside in my car, but the wrong girl appeared. She was better than nothing, and, I might add, a lot less trouble than you would have been. She didn't ask to see my police ID and just got into the car, as good as gold."

"But why a hostage?"

"Because your messing around has forced me to leave the island. I've picked a good escape route but it won't hurt to have a hostage. It'll be even better to have three, so I'd like to thank you and your friend for blundering by, just as I was on my way to the shack to collect Makiko."

"Did you drug her?"

He nodded. "I carried her through the woods to the shack, then left her while I tried to lure you into a trap at the Boardwalk. You caused all this trouble, so you were the hostage I really wanted. But I abandoned that idea after watching the cops try their ambush."

"Were Sabrina and her brother involved in your plot?"

"Nope, but I had to laugh when they were hauled away for questioning. Sabrina's such a loudmouth she deserves it." He chuckled at the memory. "Anyway, I waited until things were quiet around Cavendish, then headed for the shack and there you were, just waiting to be taken."

Makiko opened her eyes and tried to sit up. She seemed better but I convinced her to remain under the blanket. Then I heard Aaron say, "You've made another mistake, you know."

"What's that?"

"This is an island. The police will cover the airport and ferries."

He laughed. "I'm no fool. There's one ferry they won't check because they'll think it leads to a dead end."

"What do you mean?"

"We're heading for a port called Souris. A night ferry from there heads north to the Magdalen Islands. There's nowhere to hide on them so the police won't expect me to escape in that direction with my hostages. But I've got a friend in Québec with a boat. He'll sail to the Magdalens to get me."

"And us?"

"Nope. I'll find somewhere lonely to leave you, all nicely tied up. When I'm safely in Québec I'll get a message to the police where to find you. It may take a few days, so you'll be kind of hungry, but that's the way it goes."

For a while I desperately considered escape plans, then looked at the man. "I bet you're secretly A.P. Cole."

"That second-rate talent? Don't insult my intelligence."

"Then why's he disappeared?"

He shrugged. "I couldn't care less."

"What about the blackened spoon in his locker?"

"A good detective shouldn't believe every lie she hears." He laughed. "Speaking of which, you sure got suckered about Breanne."

"Breanne?"

"That redhead who's now Marilla at the Festival." He smiled. "When you were playing detective I decided to have some fun. One evening I made an anonymous phone call to Breanne, claiming I had evidence proving she was involved with the murder. She said that was crazy, but I convinced her to meet me at Saint Ann's Church."

"Where I bet you disguised yourself with a fake beard and dirty clothes so I'd think you were a drug pusher."

He chuckled. "I chewed on some lobster until Breanne arrived, then took her outside. I knew you'd be nosy enough to follow. I produced the shiny needle to make you even more suspicious of Breanne, then insulted her until she drove away."

"But there was also a note in Breanne's dressing room about horse coming ashore. I was sure that meant heroin."

The man roared with laughter. "That worked beautifully! I'll never forget the expression on your face when you read the note. It was classic!"

I stared at him. "You were in the dressing room when I found it?"

"Of course. I deliberately spilled salt to distract you while I planted the note. I'd already written it, hoping there'd be a way to set you up."

"I can't believe what I'm hearing! You mean, you're . . ."

"Exactly." Smiling, he lifted a wig off his head to reveal thin brown hair. No longer an old man. he looked about forty-five. He took some padding from his mouth and suddenly his cheeks were different. Then the man stuck thick beetle-brows over his eyes, added some horn-rimmed glasses and grinned at me in the mirror.

"Humphrey! I should have known."

* * *

Minutes later he was still laughing. "My real name is Harry Hoolif, but I loved playing Humphrey the Hick. That s-s-stammer, and wearing a tie to the softball game, and pretending to be shy with women."

"You suckered my coach?"

"You got it, kid. Sandra was a perfect addition to

my Humphrey disguise. She even helped by foolishly telling me you'd be at Covehead Harbour."

"I'll get you for hurting her. I swear it!"

"Forget it, sweetie pie. I saw better detective work when my neighbour's dog lost a bone."

"You just confessed everything about your murder plot. Don't you care that I'll tell the police?"

"By the time you talk to the cops I'll be in a new disguise and safely in hiding. They'll never find me."

"Those disguises changed everything about you except your weight. But I was fooled because your eyes were green and the Mountie's blue. I never thought of contacts."

He chuckled. "At the softball game I had green eyes, but backstage at the musical they'd become blue. You didn't notice that, eh? I had to wear the blue contacts because I'd lost the clear ones and I needed to see for my job."

"Know something else? When I first went backstage your stammer was missing. I guess you forgot to use it."

He shrugged. "Nobody's perfect."

As I looked out at the passing night I thought about talking to him at the memorial service. "You mentioned the Mountie's eyeshadow, but supposedly you weren't at Green Gables when she was investigating. So how'd you know her makeup was lavender?"

"I also accidentally mentioned the butter churn clue to you. I kicked myself afterwards over that one." He yawned. "But so what? Like I said earlier, women make useless detectives. I was never worried about getting caught."

"Know something?" Aaron said. "I think you're really dumb to underestimate Liz. She's a great detective."

Harry Hoolif didn't reply, but I gave Aaron a grateful smile. I looked at Makiko, who seemed a lot better, then focussed my attention on getting us out of this mess. But I couldn't think of anything until lights appeared ahead and I saw we were approaching a gas station.

Suddenly I had an idea. My scheme was risky but it might save us.

12

Leaning forward, I looked at Harry Hoolif. "I'm desperate. You've got to stop the car!"

"Why?" he asked suspiciously.

"I need a washroom *right now*."

Aaron nodded. "Me too."

"I too," Makiko added in a weak voice. "Please, sir." For a moment the man wavered, then he pulled into the gas station. "First I'll tank up this car, then we'll find you a washroom." As an attendant walked toward us Harry Hoolif slipped his gun under the front seat. "Remember I've got this thing handy. I've killed before, and I'll do it again if there's trouble. So don't make a sound."

"You can trust us."

He laughed. "Sure, as much as I could trust a hungry boa constrictor." Rolling down the window he gave his order to the attendant, who stared into the empty night while the fuel ran into the car. They discussed the fog, while Harry Hoolif pulled out his wallet to pay, then the attendant said the washroom was around the side of the building.

"Listen carefully," Harry Hoolif said as he parked beside the washroom door. "Take turns going inside. If there's any trouble someone gets hurt bad. I mean that."

Makiko left the car first, walking on shaky legs to the washroom. We were parked in the shadow of the building so there was no chance the attendant would see her, let alone notice she was Japanese like the missing girl on all the news reports. When she returned Aaron hurried inside, then it was my turn.

I walked straight to the building and closed the door. As I suspected, the washroom didn't connect to the rest of the service station so I couldn't alert the attendant. But I still had a plan. During the short time I was in there I used a bar of dirty soap to scrawl on the mirror *Kidnapped kids in rental car heading for Souris—phone police* then went outside. Walking to the front of the building I saw the attendant returning to his office from a car he'd just fueled.

"Hey sir," I called. "I couldn't turn off the tap. Sorry, but there's water flooding everywhere."

The man swore angrily, then ran inside, grabbed some tools and headed for the washroom. Avoiding Harry Hoolif's eyes I got into the back seat. He reversed away from the building and was changing gears when there was a shout.

The attendant had run from the washroom. "Come back!"

I wondered if Harry Hoolif would make a break for safety but instead he rolled down his window. "What's the problem, friend?"

"That girl was lying! There's no water, but she's scribbled soap all over the mirror. Make her clean up the mess!"

As the man walked angrily away, Harry Hoolif looked at me. "A message for the cops, maybe? Try another trick like that, Little Miss Detective, and it'll be your last. Now go clean it up."

* * *

We continued on in silence, until Harry Hoolif pulled into a deserted side road and stopped. He reached into the glove compartment to pop open the trunk lid, and got out with the gun.

"What's he doing?" Aaron whispered the moment the door closed.

"Probably changing his disguise. I think he keeps them in the trunk."

The night was totally black so I couldn't see him. Praying that he also couldn't see me, I took out the soap I'd saved from the washroom and leaned across Makiko. I'd just finished with the soap when Harry Hoolif returned, dressed as a Mountie. As he started the car I said, "I wish I'd noticed earlier that you knew about my Dad being a police officer. A stranger couldn't have known that kind of detail about my family." I stared at the night in moody silence, then asked, "Why'd you want the map when we stopped at the phone booth?"

"I planned to pick somewhere really remote and tell the MacNeills you were heading there. The police would have gone in that direction, giving us time to reach Souris and board the ferry."

I looked at my watch. "What time does it sail?"

"Two in the morning."

Time was running out for us. I could see lights glowing ahead in the fog and realized we were approaching Souris. Harry Hoolif ordered Makiko to lie on the floor under the blanket, then we drove through the empty streets to the ferry terminal.

A lot of cars were boarding the big vessel, which was called the *Lucy Maud Montgomery*. I could hear the blasting of a fog horn from somewhere close by and saw a lighthouse beam struggling against the murky darkness, but it was impossible to believe any ship could move safely on such a night.

"The ferry will never sail," I said. "The fog's too thick."

"Never heard of radar?"

We drove across the parking lot, then bumped up a ramp into the ferry. A number of deckhands were directing cars, but nobody paid any attention to us. Harry Hoolif killed the engine, then leaned back with a smile. "You might as well relax, kids. The trip takes five hours and we're staying right here."

"What about Makiko? She can't stay under the blanket that long."

"Want a bet?"

I gave him a dirty look, then stared at the other passengers heading above. They'd be able to eat a meal or relax in the lounge, but we were trapped here. A few people glanced our way and I noticed a couple of them whispering together, but the car deck was empty by the time the ferry's vibrations told me we were moving.

A short time later a man wearing the uniform of a ship's officer approached, motioning for Harry Hoolif to roll down his window. "Sorry to bother you, sir. I'm the ferry's second mate. A passenger asked me to investigate something."

"What?"

Stepping back from the car, the officer pointed at the window directly behind Harry Hoolif. He twisted around, then his eyes narrowed when he saw the big letters written in soap on the window: HELP. "That's, uh, nothing. Just my daughter's idea of a joke."

"You're a Mountie?"

"That's correct."

"Perhaps you'd show me your identification. I'm sure you'll understand. We're all very concerned about the missing Japanese girl."

Harry Hoolif shook his head. "I'm investigating a matter of national security. I'm forbidden to reveal my identity to anyone."

"Your daughter is assisting the investigation?"

"That's correct, and this is my son."

The mate studied Aaron's face, then looked at me. As he did, I flicked my eyes toward the floor. Leaning close to the window the man said, "What's under that blanket?"

"Nothing much." Harry Hoolif bent forward. "What's under this seat is more interesting." Producing the gun, he aimed it at Aaron. "If there's trouble I'll shoot this boy."

"Don't be foolish," the mate said. "Set these kids free, right now."

"Are you crazy? They're my hostages." He motioned at Aaron to get out of the car, then turned to me. "You and Makiko come, too. We're all going to the bridge."

* * *

Outside, on deck, the air was cold. The ferry was moving slowly through the fog, which pressed close all around. As the mate led us to a door I could hear the blasting horn and see the distant beam of the lighthouse guarding the port we'd left. When the door opened light spilled out, and I saw the Captain and several crew members. Their faces were shocked as Harry Hoolif waved the gun at them, then destroyed the radio with a couple of shots.

"I'd hate you to alert the cops, Captain." Smiling, he walked to the radar and smashed it with the gun butt. "I guess you might have tried returning to port, but that would be difficult without radar. Correct?"

"Yes," the Captain said, "but now we also can't sail to the Magdalens."

"Thanks to this meddling girl I'm no longer going there. The cops would be swarming all over those islands before I could get away. I'll have to return to Souris, then figure a way to reach the mainland from PEI."

"Without the radar we can't get back to port. You're stuck out here at sea, so let the kids go. I'm sure the courts will be fair to you."

"That's hard to believe when I've just murdered someone." He shook his head. "No, I'm not going back to prison. These kids are my ticket to freedom, so they're going ashore with me."

"But how?"

"Don't worry, I've figured that out."

* * *

Soon after we were on deck watching as huge chains were released and the ship's anchors dropped to the sea bed. The captain had used the ferry's intercom to warn passengers to remain inside, so the decks were deserted as Harry Hoolif led two members of the crew from lifeboat to lifeboat, forcing them to wreck each one's motor. Finally only one working lifeboat remained, and it was lowered to the sea.

Inside sat Harry Hoolif and the three of us.

He ordered us to throw off the lines, then started the lifeboat's engine and we slipped clear of the ferry. Through the fog I could see the faint lights of the bridge far above. There was no way the captain could have saved us but I still felt terribly alone as we moved slowly away into the night and the ferry was swallowed by the fog.

Small waves splashed away from our bow while the lifeboat chugged through the night. Ahead of us was the sweeping beam of the lighthouse guarding the harbour entrance. The regular blasting of the foghorn was a powerful sound, echoing through the night. Then, in between the blasts, I heard another sound.

The distant clanking of chains.

Harry Hoolif looked in the direction we'd come. "That captain's pulling a double-cross. He's raising the anchors. I can hear the chains."

"Is he going on to the Magdalen Islands?"

"Of course not. I bet the ferry's going back into port to alert the police."

"But the captain can't do that. The radar's destroyed."

Harry Hoolif looked at the nearby lighthouse beam. "He knows the harbour mouth is located to the left of that lighthouse. The beam will guide him back to port." He chuckled. "I think I'll fix a little surprise for that double-crosser."

"What do you mean?"

"No way I'm telling you anything more. You're smarter than I thought."

"Don't do anything dangerous," Aaron said. "There's lots of passengers on that ferry."

"My heart is breaking."

Suddenly big rocks appeared ahead. Harry Hoolif guided the lifeboat between them, then I heard pebbles grind under the hull as we ran up on shore. We climbed out of the boat, and hurried across a stony beach that was slippery with seaweed. The foghorn was so loud I wanted to cover my ears, but I needed my hands to steady myself as we began climbing a steep path. Rocks and pebbles were knocked loose by our feet, bouncing down into the foggy darkness. Finally we reached the lighthouse.

At its base was a wooden door with a big padlock. If I'd thought this would prevent Harry Hoolif from getting inside, I was wrong. One quick shot blasted it to bits and he pushed us through the doorway. Out of a small window I could see the beam sweeping the night sky. Above me a bare lightbulb hung from the high ceiling. To the left wooden stairs spiralled up into the darkness, and to the right there was a small room with red and green lights winking from electrical equipment. Harry Hoolif closed the outside door, then studied the equipment for a few seconds before reaching for a lever and pulling it down.

Immediately the beam outside and the foghorn died.

At the same time the lightbulb went out, cut off from electricity when Harry Hoolif pulled the lever. We were in total darkness. Grabbing Makiko and Aaron, I darted towards the stairs. As we scrambled up, I could hear our footsteps echoing from the circular walls.

At a landing we paused, listening for sounds of pursuit. For a moment there was silence, then an eerie whisper came up the stairs. "I'm going to get you," the voice said. Then more silence, followed by feet climbing toward us.

Squinting my eyes, I saw stairs snaking higher into the darkness. Trying not to make any noise we climbed to another landing, but found nowhere to hide. My heart was pounding with fear as Makiko pulled a fire extinguisher loose from its mounting on the wall. Then she gestured to go higher.

The walls closed around as we climbed. Makiko paused, then I heard a *phsssssssst* sound, followed by a dull clank as she put down the fire extinguisher. "*Ganbatte,*" she whispered, motioning toward the circular room directly above. In it was the huge brass lantern that had died when Harry Hoolif pulled the electrical lever. I could feel the warmth of the lantern on my face as I squeezed past to a window overlooking the night.

"The ferry!" Aaron whispered. "It's coming this way."

The ship's lights glowed through the fog, moving straight at us. "The captain won't be able to stop! The ferry's going to . . ."

At that moment there was a terrible cry, followed by the crashing of a body down the wooden stairs. "He's slipped on the extinguisher foam!" I gave Makiko a huge grin, then turned toward the stairs. "Come on, let's try to get his gun."

Holding the railing we slipped and slid down the foamy stairs to find Harry Hoolif sprawled on the landing. He was out cold. "I'll cover him," Aaron said, picking up the gun. "You two get the electricity started!"

Down and down the spiral stairs we rushed, our feet thundering in the silent air. Finally we saw the winking lights of the electrical equipment and seized the lever. As the lighthouse beam and the foghorn sprang into life I grabbed Makiko's arm. "Outside, fast!"

Hurrying through the door, we ran to see the ferry's lights. It was still coming toward the lighthouse, its emergency horn wailing, but then the ship began to change direction and we knew it would avoid running ashore. Turning to Makiko, I grinned.

"We did it! That'll teach Harry Hoolif a good lesson about female detectives."

"Is wonderful moment." Then she smiled. "I believe famous Maud would be proud of us."

"You betcha!"

13

People were thrilled by Makiko's safe return.

Her picture was everywhere—newspapers, television—and I'm proud to say some also showed Aaron and me. We were all feeling great, then Mr. Tanaka put the icing on the cake by inviting everyone to a party at Shaw's Hotel.

Not just a party but a celebration. All the guests were wearing their finest clothes. I'd found a white old-fashioned bonnet with long trailing blue ribbons, and a sundress that everyone said looked great. Makiko was in a traditional Japanese kimono, so lots of pictures were taken that afternoon.

And did we eat! In between draping our arms around each other for the cameras, we managed to find our way to the long tables on the lawn spread with a feast of seafood and salads and cheeses and desserts like lemon whip and strawberry shortcake.

Mr. Isaac, the TV producer, was sitting on a shady bench with his plate piled high. "Did you once date Miss Martin?" I asked him.

"It's true what people say: you're quite the detective. Yes, years ago in Ontario we were engaged. Then she sent Harry Hoolif to prison, not for justice but because she wanted the reward money. Until then I thought I loved Molly but after that, I just didn't know any more. We split up and I moved to Manitoba. I had no idea where she was until I arrived in PEI and saw her on stage as Marilla. You can imagine my surprise."

"But why did you go to the Mystery Weekend? I remember you arriving late at the cemetery that first night, and how shocked she was. Why'd you hurt her like that?"

He gave me a strange look. "You know, I never thought of it in those terms. I figured I'd already paid for my ticket so I intended to enjoy the weekend. Plus it was useful for my research."

Just then my coach appeared. "You're looking a bit glum," she said to Mr. Isaac with a smile. "Try some of the chilled salmon. It'll take away the worst case of the blues." We watched him head for the nearest food table, then wandered together across the lawn. Sandra knelt beside a bed of flowers that looked like pink daisies. "These are asters. Island people call them 'farewell summer.'" For a moment she was silent. "I'm awfully glad you and Makiko are back safe and sound but I must admit this whole episode with Humphrey has left me pretty unhappy."

"I'm sorry it had to work out like this. I could tell that you really liked him."

"Know something strange? Humphrey's disappeared, gone like a perfect bubble bursting in the air. He was so corny but I really liked him. That guy who kidnapped you and Makiko was another person entirely so I've still got my memories of Humphrey."

"You'll meet someone else, coach."

She smiled. "You sound like my mom." Standing up, she brushed dirt off her hands. "You know Liz, I loved everything about life before I met Humphrey and I'll love it all again."

As we returned to the party I saw that Aaron had finally arrived. "I just came from Green Gables," he said. "It's open again and I've got great news. My uncle's been hired to work there."

I was so pleased for Aaron that I hugged him. Not that I needed an excuse! Then we held hands as we crossed the lawn to join Makiko at the table of goodies. I was suddenly hungry again, and was just going after more strawberry shortcake when Aaron picked up a plate of shells.

They weren't empty.

"Aaron, I have a horrible feeling those are oysters I'm looking at."

"Good work! Austen the Great Detective strikes again."

"And I have this *really* horrible feeling that . . ."

He beamed. "Just try one, Liz. Pretty please."

Makiko giggled. "Liz-san most distressed. Is not fan of raw seafood."

"Please, Liz. I'll adore you forever."

"Well . . ." Surely a simple little oyster wouldn't hurt. But raw? Slowly I raised a shell, staring at the dark and slippery thing inside. "I'm not sure . . ." Again I hesitated but I knew it had to be done. Closing my eyes, I tilted the shell. As the oyster slipped into my mouth I shuddered, then swallowed fast. The thing slithered down my throat and then I opened my eyes, amazed. "I did it! I did it!"

Makiko applauded and cheered, and Aaron gave me a wonderful hug. Some people came over, attracted by the excitement, and demanded I repeat with another oyster. "No way," I said. "Once is enough." For a while I talked to Makiko and Aaron, then he joined 'Cameron of the Yard' and Matthew for a visit while I concentrated my attention on the "Singing Strings," a group of local musicians from high school and university. The bows of their instruments flashed back and forth in the sunlight as they played a few classics by the Beatles, and some Bach that made my skin tingle.

Then finally Mr. Beach arrived.

"Please," Makiko whispered as I hurried her across the lawn toward Mr. Beach, "why call him such? Is not his name."

"He's so gorgeous I picture him on a California beach." I watched A.P. Cole as he shook hands with various guests, then led his girlfriend Jeni to the food. "I recommend the cold lobster," I said brightly, moving in next to him. "It's so very toothsome."

He smiled. "Been browsing through your dictionary lately?"

"I have a confession to make. You were a major

suspect. That's why we followed Jeni through Charlottetown." I looked at her. "I hope you'll accept my apology."

"Of course."

She gave me such a warm smile I realized I'd judged her unfairly. But it was also true we'd been deceived by the letter she'd removed from A.P. Cole's boarding house so I asked why she'd taken it. "When he's away I collect his mail and keep it safe," Jeni explained.

"But why'd you go into the haunted church?"

"That's the one I attend, so I knew it would be pretty dark and I could give you the slip. Then I decided on a scare, just to make sure you'd leave me alone. Being a suspect kind of choked me."

I looked at A.P. Cole. "When you booked off sick from the musical I was convinced you weren't ill."

"You were right. I flew to New York City for some auditions. It was my chance to break through in the States but I couldn't risk being fired from the musical for skipping out of a week's worth of shows. That's why I pretended to be sick." Suddenly he beamed. "Want to hear some exciting news? My agent just phoned. I've landed a role down there!"

"Fabulous. What'll you be doing?"

"I'm signed for a new soap opera called *One Brave Heart*."

"Sounds great."

"I'll send you my autographed picture." He smiled at Makiko. "You guys make fantastic TV sets in Japan but what about watching them? Do you have soap operas?"

"But yes. Is favourite activity."

"Then you'll also receive a picture. Tell all your friends to be watching!"

"I am most happy for you, Cole-san."

We watched the happy couple walk away, then smiled at each other. "I've also got a confession for you, Makiko. For a while I actually suspected your dad was involved in Miss Martin's death."

"How so!"

"In Breanne's dressing room I saw the fake note saying horse had come ashore at North Lake."

"Ah! Is place of business of honoured father."

"Exactly, and I thought horse was a code word for heroin so you can understand my confusion. I guess it was just a fluke that Harry Hoolif used North Lake in the note." I smiled. "It's nice to know that guy's behind bars, but maybe he'll be bored. I should send him a few books about Nancy Drew and Miss Marple."

"Exploits of such female detectives would cause him to cough."

"No, no," I said, laughing. "You mean he'd choke. You'd better stay in Canada a few more months and I'll teach you the difficult words."

"How I would love this."

"I missed a major clue, you know. When I first met Humphrey at the softball game I noticed his dirty car belching blue exhaust. Later Alvin said that's a sign of an oil burner, but I'd forgotten this connection when the fake drug pusher drove away from Saint Ann's in a car that was both filthy and an oil burner." I paused, thinking. "Know another connection? Humphrey was fat and so was the old man, and the Mountie." I pointed at the hotel's office window. "In there the blond officer mentioned the initial on the contact lens case wasn't necessarily an I. With the case turned it was a fancy H, the first initial of both Humphrey and Harry Hoolif."

The party continued into the evening, when a fiddler arrived for a dance inside the hotel. The music was amazing, spinning us around the floor as I whirled with Aaron and other guests in jigs and reels and polkas. Aaron and I arranged to spend the next day together, but I had to say goodbye to Makiko at the party because she was leaving for Japan on an early flight.

"I'll really miss you," I said as we exchanged addresses, then I handed her a small gift. "I hope this will always be a reminder of our time together."

My present was a red-headed doll wearing a pin that said *Anne*. Makiko smiled and squeezed my hand, then produced a delicately wrapped package. When I removed the tissue I saw a wooden black-haired doll in a colourful kimono. "Is *kokeshi* doll," Makiko said. "This gift say, Liz I like you."

I stared at her. "Hey! You didn't call me Liz-san."

Makiko bowed her head shyly. "At last we are true kindred spirits."

I grinned. "Now I'll have to visit Japan for sure."

"Wonderful! This brings me great happiness." She smiled. "Will be most exciting as we stroll streets of Kyoto and people are pointing and saying, 'Look, there you see the famous Green Gables detectives.' "

Eric Wilson at Green Gables

GORD JOHNSTON PHOTO; COURTESY PEI DEPT. OF TOURISM

Eric Wilson is known for his careful research "on location" for each of his mysteries. During a summer of exploring Prince Edward Island he found many fascinating facts and locations that were perfect for *The Green Gables Detectives*, but one discovery didn't find its way into this book: a spelling error on the tombstone of L.M. Montgomery. Always one to enjoy challenging his readers, Eric invites you to detect the error when you visit the scenes of this story.

THE ST. ANDREWS WEREWOLF

A Liz Austen Mystery

ERIC WILSON

Up by the entrance of the hotel, the moonlight showed a creature. Its face had scary red eyes, a snout and jagged teeth . . .
Makiko stared at me. "Werewolf!"

When Liz Austen lands a role in a summer production of "Annie" in St. Andrews, New Brunswick, she discovers that an upcoming vote on the town's future may ruin its charm and tradition. She also meets Emily, who desperately needs a good friend to help her discover her own strength and courage.

Liz and her friend Makiko find themselves investigating the legend of the St. Andrews Werewolf, a series of arsons and a mysterious mansion on an island where time has stood still. Most importantly, they learn to search for the truth hidden beneath the surface.

"I was reading *The St. Andrews Werewolf* in bed and my Mom kept yelling, 'Turn off the light, put the book down.' But I can never put down a good book."
—*Anushka A., Scarborough, Ontario*